SHORT STORIES

OF

E. F. BENSON

British Library Cataloguing-in-Publication Data
A catalogue record for this book is available from the
British Library

CONTENTS

E.F. BENSON

Edward Frederic Benson was born at Wellington College (where his father was headmaster) in Berkshire, England in 1867. He was educated at Marlborough College, where he proved himself as an excellent athlete, representing England at figure skating, and published his first novel, *Dodo* (1893), when he was 26. The novel was quite popular, and Benson eventually expanded it into a trilogy (*Dodo the Second*, in 1914, and *Dodo Wonders*, in 1921). Nowadays, Benson is principally known for his 'Mapp and Lucia' series about Emmeline "Lucia" Lucas and Elizabeth Mapp. The series consists of six novels and two short stories, and remains popular to this day, being serialized for Radio 4 as recently as 2008. Benson was also a respected writer of ghost stories – indeed, H. P. Lovecraft spoke very highly of him, especially his story 'The Man Who Went Too Far'. Benson died of throat cancer in 1940, aged 72.

SHORT STORIES
E.F. Benson

THE ROOM IN THE TOWER

It is probable that everybody who is at all a constant dreamer has had at least one experience of an event or sequence of circumstances which have come to his mind in sleep being subsequently realized in the material world. But, in my opinion, so far from this being a strange thing, it would be far odder if this fulfilment did not occasionally happen, since our dreams are, as a rule, concerned with people whom we know and places with which we are familiar, such as might very naturally occur in the awake and day-lit world. True, these dreams are often broken into by some absurd and fantastic

incident, which puts them out of court in regard to their sub-
sequent fulfilment, but on the mere calculation of chances, it
does not appear in the least unlikely that a dream imagined
by anyone who dreams constantly should occasionally come
true. Not long ago, for instance, I experienced such a fulfilment of a dream which seems to me in no way remarkable
and to have no kind of psychical significance. The manner of
it was as follows.

A certain friend of mine, living abroad, is amiable enough
to write to me about once in a fortnight. Thus, when fourteen
days or thereabouts have elapsed since I last heard from him,
my mind, probably, either consciously or subconsciously, is
expectant of a letter from him. One night last week I dreamed
that as I was going upstairs to dress for dinner I heard, as I
often heard, the sound of the postman's knock on my front
door, and diverted my direction downstairs instead. There,
among other correspondence, was a letter from him. Thereafter the fantastic entered, for on opening it I found inside the
ace of diamonds, and scribbled across it in his well-known
handwriting, 'I am sending you this for safe custody, as you
know it is running an unreasonable risk to keep aces in Italy.'
The next evening I was just preparing to go upstairs to dress
when I heard the postman's knock, and did precisely as I had
done in my dream. There, among other letters, was one from
my friend. Only it did not contain the ace of diamonds. Had

it done so, I should have attached more weight to the matter, which, as it stands, seems to me a perfectly ordinary coincidence. No doubt I consciously or subconsciously expected a letter from him, and this suggested to me my dream. Similarly, the fact that my friend had not written to me for a fortnight suggested to him that he should do so. But occasionally it is not so easy to find such an explanation, and for the following story I can find no explanation at all. It came out of the dark, and into the dark it has gone again.

All my life I have been a habitual dreamer: the nights are few, that is to say, when I do not find on awaking in the morning that some mental experience has been mine, and sometimes, all night long, apparently, a series of the most dazzling adventures befall me. Almost without exception these adventures are pleasant, though often merely trivial. It is of an exception that I am going to speak.

It was when I was about sixteen that a certain dream first came to me, and this is how it befell. It opened with my being set down at the door of a big red-brick house, where, I understood, I was going to stay. The servant who opened the door told me that tea was going on in the garden, and led me through a low dark-panelled hall, with a large open fireplace, on to a cheerful green lawn set round with flower beds. There were grouped about the tea-table a small party of people, but they were all strangers to me except one, who was a school-fellow called Jack Stone, clearly the son of the house, and he introduced me to his mother and father and a couple of sisters. I was, I remember, somewhat astonished to find myself here, for the boy in question was scarcely known to me, and I rather disliked what I knew of him: moreover, he had left school nearly a year before. The afternoon was very hot, and an intolerable oppression reigned. On the far side of the lawn ran a red-brick wall, with an iron gate in its centre, outside which stood a walnut-tree. We sat in the shadow of the house opposite a row of long windows, inside which I could see a table with cloth laid, glimmering with glass and silver. This garden front of the house was very long, and at one end of it stood a tower of three storeys, which looked to me much older than the rest of the building.

Before long, Mrs. Stone, who, like the rest of the party, had sat in absolute silence, said to me, 'Jack will show you your room: I have given you the room in the tower.'

Quite inexplicably my heart sank at her words. I felt as if I had known that I should have the room in the tower, and that it contained something dreadful and significant. Jack instantly got up, and I understood that I had to follow him. In silence we passed through the hall, and mounted a great oak staircase with many corners, and arrived at a small landing with two doors set in it. He pushed one of these open for me to enter, and without coming in himself, closed it behind me. Then I knew that my conjecture had been right: there was something awful in the room, and with the terror of nightmare growing swiftly and enveloping me, I awoke in a spasm of terror.

Now that dream or variations of it occurred to me intermittently for fifteen years. Most often it came in exactly this form, the arrival, the tea laid out on the lawn, the deadly silence succeeded by that one deadly sentence, the mounting with Jack Stone up to the room in the tower where horror dwelt, and it always came to a close in the nightmare of terror at that which was in the room, though I never saw what it was. At other times I experienced variations on this same theme. Occasionally, for instance, we would be sitting at dinner in the dining-room, into the windows of which I had looked on the first night when the dream of this house visited me, but wherever we were, there was the same silence, the same sense of dreadful oppression and foreboding. And the silence I knew would always be broken by Mrs. Stone saying to me, 'Jack will show you your room: I have given you the room in the tower.' Upon which (this was invariable) I had to follow him up the oak staircase with many corners, and enter the place that I dreaded more and more each time that I visited it in sleep. Or again, I would find myself playing cards still in silence in a drawing-room lit with immense chandeliers, that gave a blinding illumination. What the game was I have no idea; what I remember, with a sense of miserable anticipation, was that soon Mrs. Stone would get up and say to me, 'Jack will show you your room: I have given you the room in the tower.' This drawing-room where we played cards was next to the dining-room, and, as I have said, was always brilliantly illuminated, whereas the rest of the house was full of dusk and shadows. And yet, how often, in spite of those bouquets of lights, have I not pored over the cards that were dealt to me, scarcely able for some reason to see them. Their designs, too, were strange: there were no red suits, but all were black, and among them there were certain cards which were black all over. I hated and dreaded those.

As this dream continued to recur, I got to know the greater part of the house. There was a smoking-room beyond the drawing-room, at the end of a passage with a green baize door. It was always very dark there, and as often as I went there I passed somebody whom I could not see in the doorway coming out. Curious developments, too, took place in the characters that peopled the dream as might happen to living persons. Mrs. Stone, for instance, who, when I first saw her, had been black haired, became grey, and instead of rising briskly, as she had done at first when she said, 'Jack will show you your room: I have given you the room in the tower,' got up very feebly, as if strength was leaving her limbs. Jack also grew up, and became a rather ill-looking young man, with a brown moustache, while one of the sisters ceased to appear, and I understood she was married.

Then it so happened that I was not visited by this dream for six months or more, and I began to hope, in such inexplicable dread did I hold it, that it had passed away for good. But one night after this interval I again found myself being shown out on to the lawn for tea, and Mrs. Stone was not there, while the others were all dressed in black. At once I guessed the reason, and my heart leaped at the thought that perhaps this time I should not have to sleep in the room in the tower, and though we usually all sat in silence, on this occasion the sense of relief made me talk and laugh as I had never yet done. But even then matters were not altogether comfortable, for no one else spoke, but they all looked secretly at each other. And soon the foolish stream of my talk ran dry, and gradually an apprehension worse than anything I had previously known gained on me as the light slowly faded.

Suddenly a voice which I knew well broke the stillness, the voice of Mrs. Stone, saying, 'Jack will show you your room: I have given you the room in the tower.' It seemed to come from near the gate in the red-brick wall that bounded the lawn, and looking up, I saw that the grass outside was sown thick with gravestones. A curious greyish light shone from them, and I could read the lettering on the grave nearest me, and it was, 'In evil memory of Julia Stone'. And as usual Jack got up, and again I followed him through the hall and up the staircase with many corners. On this occasion it was darker than usual, and when I passed into the room in the tower I could only just see the furniture, the position of which was already familiar to me. Also there was a dreadful odour of decay in the room, and I woke screaming.

The dream, with such variations and developments as I have mentioned, went on at intervals for fifteen years. Sometimes I would dream it two or three nights in succession; once, as I have said, there was an intermission of six months, but taking a reasonable average, I should say that I dreamed it quite as often as once in a month. It had, as is plain, something of nightmare about it, since it always ended in the same appalling terror, which so far from getting less, seemed to me to gather fresh fear every time that I experienced it. There was, too, a strange and dreadful consistency about it. The characters in it, as I have mentioned, got regularly older, death and marriage visited this silent family, and I never in the dream, after Mrs. Stone had died, set eyes on her again. But it was always her voice that told me that the room in the tower was prepared for me, and whether we had tea out on the lawn, or the scene was laid in one of the rooms overlooking it, I could always see her gravestone standing just outside the iron gate. It was the same, too, with the married daughter; usually she was not present, but once or twice she returned again, in company with a man, whom I took to be her husband. He, too, like the rest of them, was always silent. But, owing to the constant repetition of the dream, I had ceased to attach, in my waking hours, any significance to it. I never met Jack Stone again during all those years, nor did I ever see a house that resembled this dark house of my dream. And then something happened.

I had been in London in this year, up till the end of July, and during the first week in August went down to stay with a friend in a house he had taken for the summer months, in the Ashdown Forest district of Sussex. I left London early, for John Clinton was to meet me at Forest Row Station, and we were going to spend the day golfing, and go to his house in the evening. He had his motor with him, and we set off, about five in the afternoon, after a thoroughly delightful day, for the drive, the distance being some ten miles. As it was still so early we did not have tea at the clubhouse, but waited till we should get home. As we drove, the weather, which up till then had been, though hot, deliciously fresh, seemed to me to alter in quality, and become very stagnant and oppressive, and I felt that indefinable sense of ominous apprehension that I am accustomed to before thunder. John, however, did not share my views, attributing my loss of lightness to the fact that I had lost both my matches. Events proved, however, that I was right, though I do not think that the thunderstorm that broke that night was the sole cause of my depression.

Our way lay through deep high-banked lanes, and before we had gone very far I fell asleep, and was only awakened by the stopping of the motor. And with a sudden thrill, partly of fear but chiefly of curiosity, I found myself standing in the doorway of my house of dreams. We went, I half wondering whether or not I was dreaming still, through a low oak-panelled hall, and out on to the lawn, where tea was laid in the shadow of the house. It was set in flower beds, a red-brick wall, with a gate in it, bounded one side and out beyond that was a space of rough grass with a walnut tree. The façade of the house was very long, and at one end stood a three-storeyed tower, markedly older than the rest.

Here for the moment all resemblance to the repeated dream ceased. There was no silent and somehow terrible family, but a large assembly of exceedingly cheerful persons, all of whom were known to me. And in spite of the horror with which the dream itself had always filled me, I felt nothing of it now that the scene of it was thus reproduced before me. But I felt the intensest curiosity as to what was going to happen.

Tea pursued its cheerful course, and before long Mrs. Clinton got up. And at that moment I think I knew what she was going to say. She spoke to me, and what she said was:

'Jack will show you your room: I have given you the room in the tower.'

At that, for half a second, the horror of the dream took

hold of me again. But it quickly passed, and again I felt nothing more than the most intense curiosity. It was not very long before it was amply satisfied.

John turned to me.

'Right up at the top of the house,' he said 'but I think you'll be comfortable. We're absolutely full up. Would you like to go and see it now? By Jove, I believe that you are right, and that we are going to have a thunderstorm. How dark it has become.'

I got up and followed him. We passed through the hall, and up the perfectly familiar staircase. Then he opened the door, and I went in. And at that moment sheer unreasoning terror again possessed me. I did not know for certain what I feared: I simply feared. Then like a sudden recollection, when one remembers a name which has long escaped the memory, I knew what I feared. I feared Mrs. Stone, whose grave with the sinister inscription, 'In evil memory', I had so often seen in my dream, just beyond the lawn which lay below my window. And then once more the fear passed so completely that I wondered what there was to fear, and I found myself, sober and quiet and sane, in the room in the tower, the name of which I had so often heard in my dream and the scene of which was so familiar.

I looked round it with a certain sense of proprietorship, and found that nothing had been changed from the dreaming nights in which I knew it so well. Just to the left of the door was the bed, lengthways along the wall, with the head of it in the angle. In a line with it was the fireplace and a small bookcase; opposite the door the outer wall was pierced by two lattice-paned windows, between which stood the dressing-table, while ranged along the fourth wall was the washing-stand and a big cupboard. My luggage had already been unpacked, for the furniture of dressing and undressing lay orderly on the washstand and toilet-table, while my dinner clothes were spread out on the coverlet of the bed. And then, with a sudden start of unexplained dismay, I saw that there were two rather conspicuous objects which I had not seen before in my dreams: one a life-sized oil-painting of Mrs. Stone, the other a black-and-white sketch of Jack Stone, representing him as he had appeared to me only a week before in the last of the series of these repeated dreams, a rather secret and evil-looking man of about thirty. His picture hung between the windows, looking straight across the room to the other portrait, which hung at the side of the bed. At that I looked next, and as I looked I felt once more the horror of nightmare seize me.

It represented Mrs. Stone as I had seen her last in my dreams: old and withered and white haired. But in spite of the evident feebleness of body, a dreadful exuberance and vitality shone through the envelope of flesh, an exuberance wholly malign, a vitality that foamed and frothed with unimaginable

14

evil. Evil beamed from the narrow, leering eyes; it laughed in the demon-like mouth. The whole face was instinct with some secret and appalling mirth; the hands, clasped together on the knee, seemed shaking with suppressed and nameless glee. Then I saw also that it was signed in the left-hand bottom corner, and wondering who the artist could be, I looked more closely, and read the inscription, 'Julia Stone by Julia Stone'.

There came a tap at the door, and John Clinton entered.

'Got everything you want?' he asked.

'Rather more than I want,' said I, pointing to the picture.

He laughed.

'Hard-featured old lady,' he said. 'By herself, too, I remember. Anyhow she can't have flattered herself much.'

'But don't you see?' said I. 'It's scarcely a human face at all. It's the face of some witch, of some devil.'

He looked at it more closely.

'Yes, it isn't very pleasant,' he said. 'Scarcely a bedside manner, eh? Yes; I can imagine getting the nightmare, if I went to sleep with that close by me. I'll have it taken down if you like.'

'I really wish you would,' I said.

He rang the bell, and with the help of a servant we detached the picture and carried it out on to the landing, and put it with its face to the wall.

'By Jove, the old lady is a weight,' said John, mopping his forehead. 'I wonder if she had something on her mind.'

The extraordinary weight of the picture had struck me too. I was about to reply, when I caught sight of my own hand. There was blood on it, in considerable quantities, covering the whole palm.

'I've cut myself somehow,' said I.

John gave a little startled exclamation.

'Why, I have too,' he said.

Simultaneously the footman took out his handkerchief and wiped his hand with it. I saw that there was blood also on his handkerchief.

John and I went back into the tower room and washed the blood off; but neither on his hand nor on mine was there the slightest trace of a scratch or cut. It seemed to me that, having ascertained this, we both, by a sort of tacit consent, did not allude to it again. Something in my case had dimly occurred to me that I did not wish to think about. It was but a conjecture, but I fancied that I knew the same thing had occurred to him.

The heat and oppression of the air, for the storm we had expected was still undischarged, increased very much after dinner, and for some time most of the party, among whom were John Clinton and myself, sat outside on the path bounding the lawn, where we had had tea. The night was absolutely

16

dark, and no twinkle of star or moon ray could penetrate the pall of cloud that overset the sky. By degrees our assembly thinned, the women went up to bed, men dispersed to the smoking-or billiard-room, and by eleven o'clock my host and I were the only two left. All the evening I thought that he had something on his mind, and as soon as we were alone he spoke.

'The man who helped us with the picture had blood on his hand, too, did you notice?' he said. 'I asked him just now if he had cut himself, and he said he supposed he had, but that he could find no mark of it. Now where did that blood come from?'

By dint of telling myself that I was not going to think about it, I had succeeded in not doing so, and I did not want, especially just at bedtime, to be reminded of it.

'I don't know,' said I, 'and I don't really care so long as the picture of Mrs. Julia Stone is not by my bed.'

He got up.

'But it's odd,' he said. 'Ha! Now you'll see another odd thing.'

A dog of his, an Irish terrier by breed, had come out of the house as we talked. The door behind us into the hall was open, and a bright oblong of light shone across the lawn to the iron gate which led on to the rough grass outside, where the walnut-tree stood. I saw that the dog had all his hackles up, bristling with rage and fright; his lips were curled back from his teeth, as if he was ready to spring at something, and he was growling to himself. He took not the slightest notice of his master or me, but stiffly and tensely walked across the grass to the iron gate. There he stood for a moment, looking through the bars and still growling. Then of a sudden his courage seemed to desert him: he gave one long howl, and scuttled back to the house with a curious crouching sort of movement.

'He does that half a dozen times a day,' said John. 'He sees something which he both hates and fears.'

I walked to the gate and looked over it. Something was moving on the grass outside, and soon a sound which I could not instantly identify came to my ears. Then I remembered what it was: it was the purring of a cat. I lit a match, and saw the purrer, a big blue Persian, walking round and round in a little circle just outside the gate, stepping high and ecstatically, with tail carried aloft like a banner. Its eyes were bright and shining, and every now and then it put its head down and sniffed at the grass.

I laughed.

'The end of that mystery, I am afraid,' I said. 'Here's a large cat having Walpurgis night all alone.'

'Yes, that's Darius,' said John. 'He spends half the day and all night there. But that's not the end of the dog mystery, for

Toby and he are the best of friends, but the beginning of the cat mystery. What's the cat doing there? And why is Darius pleased, while Toby is terror-stricken?'

At that moment I remembered the rather horrible details of my dreams when I saw through the gate, just where the cat was now, the white tombstone with the sinister inscription. But before I could answer the rain began, as suddenly and heavily as if a tap had been turned on, and simultaneously the big cat squeezed through the bars of the gate, and came leaping across the lawn to the house for shelter. Then it sat in the doorway, looking out eagerly into the dark. It spat and struck at John with its paw, as he pushed it in, in order to close the door.

Somehow, with the portrait of Julia Stone in the passage outside, the room in the tower had absolutely no alarm for me, and as I went to bed, feeling very sleepy and heavy, I had nothing more than interest for the curious incident about our bleeding hands, and the conduct of the cat and dog. The last thing I looked at before I put out my light was the square empty space by my bed where the portrait had been. Here the paper was of its original full tint of dark red: over the rest of the walls it had faded. Then I blew out my candle and instantly fell asleep.

My awakening was equally instantaneous, and I sat bolt upright in bed under the impression that some bright light had been flashed in my face, though it was now absolutely pitch dark. I knew exactly where I was, in the room which I had dreaded in dreams, but no horror that I ever felt when asleep approached the fear that now invaded and froze my brain. Immediately after a peal of thunder crackled just above the house, but the probability that it was only a flash of lightning which awoke me gave no reassurance to my galloping heart. Something I knew was in the room with me, and instinctively I put out my right hand, which was nearest the wall, to keep it away. And my hand touched the edge of a picture-frame hanging close to me.

I sprang out of bed, upsetting the small table that stood by it, and I heard my watch, candle, and matches clatter on to the floor. But for the moment there was no need of light, for a blinding flash leaped out of the clouds, and showed me that by my bed again hung the picture of Mrs. Stone. And instantly the room went into blackness again. But in that flash I saw another thing also, namely a figure that leaned over the end of my bed, watching me. It was dressed in some close-clinging white garment, spotted and stained with mould, and the face was that of the portrait.

Overhead the thunder cracked and roared, and when it ceased and the deathly stillness succeeded, I heard the rustle of movement coming nearer me, and, more horrible yet, perceived an odour of corruption and decay. And then a hand was laid on the side of my neck, and close beside my ear I heard quick-taken, eager breathing. Yet I knew that this thing, though it could be perceived by touch, by smell, by eye and by ear, was still not of this earth, but something that had passed out of the body and had power to make itself manifest. Then a voice, already familiar to me, spoke.

'I knew you would come to the room in the tower,' it said. 'I have been long waiting for you. At last you have come. To-night I shall feast; before long we will feast together.'

And the quick breathing came closer to me; I could feel it on my neck.

At that the terror, which I think had paralysed me for the moment, gave way to the wild instinct of self-preservation. I hit wildly with both arms, kicking out at the same moment, and heard a little animal-squeal, and something soft dropped with a thud beside me. I took a couple of steps forward, nearly tripping up over whatever it was that lay there, and by the merest good luck found the handle of the door. In another second I ran out on the landing, and had banged the door behind me. Almost at the same moment I heard a door open somewhere below, and John Clinton, candle in hand, came running upstairs.

'What is it?' he said. 'I sleep just below you, and heard a noise as if—Good heavens, there's blood on your shoulder.'

I stood there, so he told me afterwards, swaying from side

to side, white as a sheet, with the mark on my shoulder as if a hand covered with blood had been laid there.

'It's in there,' I said, pointing. 'She, you know. The portrait is in there, too, hanging up on the place we took it from.'

At that he laughed.

'My dear fellow, this is mere nightmare,' he said.

He pushed by me, and opened the door, I standing there simply inert with terror, unable to stop him, unable to move.

'Phew! What an awful smell,' he said.

Then there was silence; he had passed out of my sight behind the open door. Next moment he came out again, as white as myself, and instantly shut it.

'Yes, the portrait's there,' he said, 'and on the floor is a thing – a thing spotted with earth, like what they bury people in. Come away, quick, come away.'

How I got downstairs I hardly knew. An awful shuddering and nausea of the spirit rather than of the flesh had seized me, and more than once he had to place my feet upon the steps, while every now and then he cast glances of terror and apprehension up the stairs. But in time we came to his dressing-room on the floor below, and there I told him what I have here described.

The sequel can be made short; indeed, some of my readers have perhaps already guessed what it was, if they remember that inexplicable affair of the churchyard at West Fawley, some eight years ago, where an attempt was made three times to bury the body of a certain woman who had committed suicide. On each occasion the coffin was found in the course of a few days again protruding from the ground. After the third attempt, in order that the thing should not be talked about, the body was buried elsewhere in unconsecrated ground. Where it was buried was just outside the iron gate of the garden belonging to the house where this woman had lived. She had committed suicide in a room at the top of the tower in that house. Her name was Julia Stone.

Subsequently the body was again secretly dug up, and the coffin was found to be full of blood.

THE BUS CONDUCTOR

My friend, Hugh Grainger, and I had just returned from a two days' visit in the country, where we had been staying in a house of sinister repute which was supposed to be haunted by ghosts of a peculiarly fearsome and truculent sort. The house itself was all that such a house should be, Jacobean and oak-panelled, with long dark passages and high vaulted rooms. It stood, also, very remote, and was encompassed by a wood of sombre pines that muttered and whispered in the dark, and all the time that we were there a south-westerly gale with torrents of scolding rain had prevailed, so that by day and night weird voices moaned and fluted in the chimneys, a company of uneasy spirits held colloquy among the trees, and sudden tattoos and tappings beckoned from the window-panes. But in spite of these surroundings, which were sufficient in themselves, one would almost say, spontaneously to generate occult phenomena, nothing of any description had occurred. I am bound to add, also, that my own state of mind was peculiarly well adapted to receive or even to invent the sights and sounds we had gone to seek, for I was, I confess, during the whole time that we were there, in a state of abject apprehension, and lay awake both nights through hours of terrified unrest, afraid of the dark, yet more afraid of what a lighted candle might show me.

Hugh Grainger, on the evening after our return to town, had dined with me, and after dinner our conversation, as was natural, soon came back to these entrancing topics.

'But why you go ghost-seeking I cannot imagine,' he said, 'because your teeth were chattering and your eyes starting out of your head all the time you were there, from sheer fright. Or do you like being frightened?'

Hugh, though generally intelligent, is dense in certain ways; this is one of them.

'Why, of course, I like being frightened,' I said. 'I want to be made to creep and creep and creep. Fear is the most absorbing and luxurious of emotions. One forgets all else if one is afraid.'

'Well, the fact that neither of us saw anything,' he said, 'confirms what I have always believed.'

'And what have you always believed?'

'That these phenomena are purely objective, not subjective, and that one's state of mind has nothing to do with the perception that perceives them, nor have circumstances or surroundings anything to do with them either. Look at Osburton. It has had the reputation of being a haunted house for years, and it certainly has all the accessories of one. Look at yourself, too, with all your nerves on edge, afraid to look round or light a candle for fear of seeing something! Surely there was the right man in the right place then, if ghosts are subjective.'

He got up and lit a cigarette, and looking at him – Hugh is about six feet high, and as broad as he is long – I felt a retort on my lips, for I could not help my mind going back to a certain period in his life, when, from some cause which, as far as I knew, he had never told anybody, he had become a mere quivering mass of disordered nerves. Oddly enough, at the same moment and for the first time, he began, to speak of it himself.

'You may reply that it was not worth my while to go either,' he said, 'because I was so clearly the wrong man in the wrong place. But I wasn't. You for all your apprehensions and expectancy have never seen a ghost. But I have, though I am the last person in the world you would have thought likely to do so, and, though my nerves are steady enough again now, it knocked me all to bits.'

He sat down again in his chair.

'No doubt you remember my going to bits,' he said, 'and since I believe that I am sound again now, I should rather like to tell you about it. But before I couldn't; I couldn't speak of it at all to anybody. Yet there ought to have been nothing frightening about it; what I saw was certainly a most useful and friendly ghost. But it came from the shaded side of things; it looked suddenly out of the night and the mystery with which life is surrounded.

'I want first to tell you quite shortly my theory about ghost-seeing,' he continued, 'and I can explain it best by a simile, an image. Imagine then that you and I and everybody in the world are like people whose eye is directly opposite a little tiny hole in a sheet of cardboard which is continually shifting and revolving and moving about. Back to back with that sheet of cardboard is another, which also, by laws of its own, is in perpetual but independent motion. In it too there is another hole, and when, fortuitously it would seem, these two holes, the one through which we are always looking, and the other in the spiritual plane, come opposite one another, we see through, and then only do the sights and sounds of the spiritual world become visible or audible to us. With most people these holes never come opposite each other during their life. But at the hour of death they do, and then they remain stationary. That, I fancy, is how we "pass over".

'Now, in some natures, these holes are comparatively large, and are constantly coming into opposition. Clairvoyants, mediums are like that. But, as far as I knew, I had no clairvoyant or mediumistic powers at all. I therefore am the sort of person who long ago made up his mind that he never would see a ghost. It was, so to speak, an incalculable chance that my minute spy-hole should come into opposition with the other. But it did: and it knocked me out of time.'

I had heard some such theory before, and though Hugh put it rather picturesquely, there was nothing in the least convincing or practical about it. It might be so, or again it might not.

'I hope your ghost was more original than your theory,' said I, in order to bring him to the point.

'Yes, I think it was. You shall judge.'

I put on more coal and poked up the fire. Hugh has got, so I have always considered, a great talent for telling stories, and that sense of drama which is so necessary for the narrator. Indeed before now, I have suggested to him that he should take this up as a profession, sit by the fountain in Piccadilly Circus, when times are, as usual, bad, and tell stories to the passers-by in the street. Arabian fashion, for reward. The most part of mankind, I am aware, do not like long stories, but to the few, among whom I number myself, who really like to listen to lengthy accounts of experiences, Hugh is an ideal narrator. I do not care for his theories, or for his similes, but when it comes to facts, to things that happened, I like him to be lengthy.

'Go on, please, and slowly,' I said. 'Brevity may be the soul of wit, but it is the ruin of story-telling. I want to hear when and where and how it all was, and what you had for lunch and where you had dined and what –'

Hugh began:

'It was the 24th of June, just eighteen months ago,' he said. 'I had left my flat, you may remember, and come up from the country to stay with you for a week. We had dined alone here –'

I could not help interrupting.

'Did you see the ghost here?' I asked. 'In this square little box of a house in a modern street?'

'I was in the house when I saw it.'

I hugged myself in silence.

'We had dined alone here in Graeme Street,' he said, 'and after dinner I went out to some party, and you stopped at home. At dinner your man did not wait, and when I asked where he was, you told me he was ill, and, I thought, changed the subject rather abruptly. You gave me your latch-key when I went out, and on coming back, I found you had gone to bed. There were, however, several letters for me, which required answers. I wrote them there and then, and posted them at the pillar-box opposite. So I suppose it was rather late when I went upstairs.

'You had put me in the front room, on the third floor, overlooking the street, a room which I thought you generally occupied yourself. It was a very hot night, and though there had been a moon when I started to my party, on my return the whole sky was cloud-covered, and it both looked and felt as if we might have a thunderstorm before morning. I was feeling very sleepy and heavy, and it was not till after I had got into bed that I noticed by the shadows of the window-frames on the blind that only one of the windows was open. But it did not seem worth while to get out of bed in order to open the other, though I felt rather airless and uncomfortable, and I went to sleep.

'What time it was when I awoke I do not know, but it was certainly not yet dawn, and I never remember being conscious of such an extraordinary stillness as prevailed. There was no sound either of foot-passengers or wheeled traffic; the music of life appeared to be absolutely mute. But now instead of being sleepy and heavy, I felt, though I must have slept an hour or two at most, since it was still quite dark, perfectly fresh and wide-awake, and the effort which had seemed not worth making before, that of getting out of bed and open-ing the other window, was quite easy now, and I pulled up the blind, threw it wide open, and leaned out, for somehow I parched and pined for air. Even outside the oppression was very noticeable, and though, as you know, I am not easily given to feel the mental effects of climate, I was aware of an awful creepiness coming over me. I tried to analyse it away, but without success; the past day had been pleasant, I looked forward to another pleasant day tomorrow, and yet I was full of some nameless apprehension. I felt, too, dreadfully lonely in this stillness before the dawn.

'Then I heard suddenly and not very far away the sound of some approaching vehicle; I could distinguish the tread of two horses walking at a slow foot's pace. They were, though yet invisible, coming up the street, and yet this indication of life did not abate that dreadful sense of loneliness which I have spoken of. Also in some dim unformulated way that which was coming seemed to me to have something to do with the cause of my oppression.

'Then the vehicle came into sight. At first I could not distinguish what it was. Then I saw that the horses were black and had long tails, and that what they dragged was made of glass, but had a black frame. It was a hearse. Empty.

'It was moving up this side of the street. It stopped at your door.

'Then the obvious solution struck me. You had said at dinner that your man was ill, and you were, I thought, unwilling to speak more about his illness. No doubt, so I imagined now, he was dead, and for some reason, perhaps because you did not want me to know anything about it, you were having the body removed at night. This, I must tell you, passed through my mind quite instantaneously, and it did not occur to me how unlikely it really was, before the next thing happened.

'I was still leaning out of the window, and I remember

also wondering, yet only momentarily, how odd it was that I saw things – or rather the one thing I was looking at – so very distinctly. Of course, there was a moon behind the clouds, but it was curious how every detail of the hearse and the horses was visible. There was only one man, the driver, with it, and the street was otherwise absolutely empty. It was at him I was looking now. I could see every detail of his clothes, but from where I was, so high above him, I could not see his face. He had on grey trousers, brown boots, a black coat buttoned all the way up, and a straw hat. Over his shoulder there was a strap, which seemed to support some sort of little bag. He looked exactly like – well, from my description what did he look exactly like?'

'Why – a bus-conductor,' I said instantly.

'So I thought, and even while I was thinking this, he looked up at me. He had a rather long thin face, and on his left cheek there was a mole with a growth of dark hair on it. All this was as distinct as if it had been noonday, and as if I was within a yard of him. But – so instantaneous was all that takes so long in telling – I had not time to think it strange that the driver of a hearse should be so unfunereally dressed.

'Then he touched his hat to me, and jerked his thumb over his shoulder.'

' "Just room for one inside, sir," he said.

'There was something so odious, so coarse, so unfeeling

about this that I instantly drew my head in, pulled the blind down again, and then, for what reason I do not know, turned on the electric light in order to see what time it was. The hands of my watch pointed to half-past eleven.

'It was then for the first time, I think, that a doubt crossed my mind as to the nature of what I had just seen. But I put out the light again, got into bed, and began to think. We had dined; I had gone to a party, had come back and written letters, had gone to bed and had slept. So how could it be half-past eleven? . . . Or – *what* half-past eleven was it?

'Then another easy solution struck me; my watch must have stopped. But it had not; I could hear it ticking.

'There was stillness and silence again. I expected every moment to hear muffled footsteps on the stairs, footsteps moving slowly and smally under the weight of a heavy burden, but from inside the house there was no sound whatever. Outside, too, there was the same dead silence, while the hearse waited at the door. And the minutes ticked on and ticked on, and at length I began to see a difference in the light in the room, and knew that the dawn was beginning to break outside. But how had it happened then that if the corpse was to be removed at night it had not gone, and that the hearse still waited, when morning was already coming?

'Presently I got out of bed again, and with the sense of strong physical shrinking I went to the window and pulled back the blind. The dawn was coming fast; the whole street was lit by that silver hueless light of morning. But there was no hearse there.

'Once again I looked at my watch. It was just a quarter-past four. But I would swear that not half an hour had passed since it had told me that it was half-past eleven.

'Then a curious double sense, as if I was living in the present and at the same moment had been living in some other time, came over me. It was dawn on June 25th, and the street, as natural, was empty. But a little while ago the driver of a hearse had spoken to me, and it was half-past eleven. What was that driver, to what plane did he belong? And again *what* half-past eleven was it that I had seen recorded on the dial of my watch?

'And then I told myself that the whole thing had been a dream. But if you ask me whether I believed what I told myself, I must confess that I did not.

'Your man did not appear at breakfast next morning, nor did I see him again before I left that afternoon. I think if I had, I should have told you about all this, but it was still possible, you see, that what I had seen was a real hearse, driven by a real driver, for all the ghastly gaiety of the face that had looked up to mine, and the levity of his pointing hand. I might pos-sibly have fallen asleep soon after seeing him, and slumbered through the removal of the body and the departure of the hearse. So I did not speak of it to you.'

There was something wonderfully straightforward and pro-saic in all this; here were not Jacobean houses oak-panelled and surrounded by weeping pine-trees, and somehow the very absence of suitable surroundings made the story more impress-ive. But for a moment a doubt assailed me.

'Don't tell me it was all a dream,' I said.

'I don't know whether it was or not. I can only say that I believe myself to have been wide awake. In any case the rest of the story is – odd.'

'I went out of town again that afternoon,' he continued, 'and I may say that I don't think that even for a moment did I get the haunting sense of what I had seen or dreamed that night out of my mind. It was present to me always as some vision unfulfilled. It was as if some clock had struck the four quarters, and I was still waiting to hear what the hour would be.

'Exactly a month afterwards I was in London again, but only for the day. I arrived at Victoria about eleven, and took the Underground to Sloane Square in order to see if you were in town and would give me lunch. It was a baking hot morn-ing, and I intended to take a bus from the King's Road as far as Graeme Street. There was one standing at the corner just as I came out of the station, but I saw that the top was full, and the inside appeared to be full also. Just as I came up to it the conductor who, I suppose, had been inside, collecting fares or what not, came out on to the step within a few feet of me. He wore grey trousers, brown boots, a black coat buttoned, a straw hat, and over his shoulder was a strap on which hung his little machine for punching tickets. I saw his face, too; it was the face of the driver of the hearse, with a mole on the left cheek. Then he spoke to me, jerking his thumb over his shoulder.

' "Just room for one inside, sir," he said.

'At that a sort of panic-terror took possession of me, and I knew I gesticulated wildly with my arms, and cried, "No, no!" But at that moment I was living not in the hour that was then passing, but in that hour which had passed a month ago, when I leaned from the window of your bedroom here just before the dawn broke. At this moment, too, I knew that my spy-hole had been opposite the spy-hole into the spiritual world. What I had seen there had some significance, now being fulfilled, beyond the significance of the trivial happenings of today and tomorrow. The Powers of which we know so little were visibly working before me. And I stood there on the pavement shaking and trembling.

'I was opposite the post-office at the corner, and just as the bus started my eye fell on the clock in the window there. I need not tell you what the time was.

'Perhaps I need not tell you the rest, for you probably conjecture it, since you will not have forgotten what happened at the corner of Sloane Square at the end of July, the summer before last. The bus pulled out from the pavement into the street in order to get round a van that was standing in front of it. At the moment there came down the King's Road a big motor going at a hideously dangerous pace. It crashed full into the bus, burrowing into it as a gimlet burrows into a board.'

He paused.

'And that's my story,' he said.

BAGNELL TERRACE

I had been for ten years an inhabitant of Bagnell Terrace, and, like all those who have been so fortunate as to secure a footing there, was convinced that for amenity, convenience, and tranquillity it is unrivalled in the length and breadth of London. The houses are small; we could, none of us, give an evening party or a dance, but we who live in Bagnell Terrace do not desire to do anything of the kind. We do not go in for sounds of revelry at night, nor, indeed, is there much revelry during the day, for we have gone to Bagnell Terrace in order to be anchored in a quiet little backwater. There is no traffic through it, for the terrace is a cul-de-sac, closed at the far end by a high brick wall, along which, on summer nights, cats trip lightly on visits to their friends. Even the cats of Bagnell Terrace have caught something of its discretion and tranquillity, for they do not hail each other with long-drawn yells of mortal agony like their cousins in less well-conducted places, but sit and have quiet little parties like the owners of the houses in which they condescend to be lodged and boarded.

But, though I was more content to be in Bagnell Terrace than anywhere else, I had not got, and was beginning to be afraid I never should get the particular house which I coveted above all others. This was at the top end of the terrace adjoining the wall that closed it, and in one respect it was unlike the other houses, which so much resemble each other. The others have little square gardens in front of them, where we have our bulbs abloom in the spring, when they present a very gay appearance, but the gardens are too small, and London too sunless to allow of any very effective horticulture. The house, however, to which I had so long turned envious eyes, had no garden in front of it; instead, the space had been used for the erection of a big, square room (for a small garden will make a very well-sized room) connected with the house by a covered passage. Rooms in Bagnell Terrace, though sunny and cheerful, are not large, and just one big room, so it occurred to me, would give the final touch of perfection to those delightful little residences.

Now, the inhabitants of this desirable abode were something of a mystery to our neighbourly little circle; though we knew that a man lived there (for he was occasionally seen leaving or entering his house), he was personally unknown to us. A curious point was that, though we had all (though rarely) encountered him on the pavements, there was a considerable discrepancy in the impression he had made on us. He certainly walked briskly, as if the vigour of life was still his, but while I believed that he was a young man, Hugh Abbot, who lived in the house next his, was convinced that, in spite of his briskness, he was not only old, but very old. Hugh and I, lifelong bachelor friends, often discussed him in the ramble of conversation when he had dropped in for an after-dinner pipe, or I had gone across for a game of chess. His name was not known to us, so, by reason of my desire for his house, we called him Naboth. We both agreed that there was something odd about him, something baffling and elusive.

I had been away for a couple of months one winter in Egypt; the night after my return Hugh dined with me, and after dinner I produced those trophies which the strongest-minded are unable to refrain from purchasing, when they are offered by an engaging burnoused ruffian in the Valley of the Tombs of the Kings. There were some beads (not quite so blue as they had appeared there), a scarab or two, and for the last I kept the piece of which I was really proud, namely, a small lapis-lazuli statuette, a few inches high, of a cat. It sat square and stiff on its haunches, with upright forelegs, and, in spite of the small scale, so good were the proportions and so accurate the observation of the artist, that it gave the impression of being much bigger. As it stood on Hugh's palm it was certainly small, but if, without the sight of it, I pictured it to myself, it represented itself as far larger than it really was.

"And the odd thing is," I said, "that though it is far and away the best thing I picked up, I cannot for the life of me remember where I bought it. Somehow I feel that I've always had it."

He had been looking very intently at it. Then he jumped up from his chair and put it down on the chimney-piece.

"I don't think I quite like it," he said, "and I can't tell you why. Oh, a jolly bit of workmanship; I don't mean that. And you can't remember where you got it, did you say? That's odd . . . Well, what about a game of chess?"

We played a couple of games, without much concentration or fervour, and more than once I saw him glance with a puzzled look at my little image on the chimney-piece. But he said nothing more about it, and when our games were over he gave me the discursive news of the Terrace. A house had fallen vacant and been instantly snapped up.

"Not Naboth's?" I asked.

"No, not Naboth's. Naboth is in possession still. Very much in possession; going strong."

"Anything new?" I asked.

"Oh, just bits of things. I've seen him a good many times lately, and yet I can't get any clear idea of him. I met him three days ago, as I was coming out of my gate, and had a good look at him, and for a moment I agreed with you and thought he was a young man. Then he turned and stared me in the face for a second, and I thought I had never seen anyone so old. Frightfully alive, but more than old – antique, primeval."

"And then?" I asked.

"He passed on, and I found myself, as has so often happened before, quite unable to remember what his face was like. Was he old or young? I didn't know. What was his mouth like, or his nose? But it was the question of his age which was the most baffling."

Hugh stretched his feet out towards the blaze, and sank back in his chair, with one more frowning look at my lapis lazuli cat.

"Though after all, what is age?" he said. "We measure age by time, we say 'so many years', and forget that we're in eternity here and now, just as we say we're in a room or in Bagnell Terrace, though we're much more truly in infinity."

"What has that got to do with Naboth?" I asked.

Hugh beat his pipe out against the bars of the grate before he answered.

"Well, it will probably sound quite cracked to you," he said, "unless Egypt, the land of ancient mystery, has softened your rind of materialism, but it struck me then that Naboth belonged to eternity much more obviously than we do. We belong to it, of course; we can't help that; but he's less involved in this error or illusion of time than we are. Dear me, it sounds amazing nonsense when I put it into words."

I laughed.

"I'm afraid my rind of materialism isn't soft enough yet,"

I said. "What you say implies that you think Naboth is a sort of apparition, a ghost, a spirit of the dead that manifests itself as a human being, though it isn't one!"

He drew his legs up to him again.

"Yes; it must be nonsense," he said. "Besides, he has been so much in evidence lately, and we can't all be seeing a ghost. It doesn't happen. And there have been noises coming from his house, loud and cheerful noises, which I've never heard before. Somebody plays an instrument like a flute in that big, square room you envy so much, and somebody beats an accompaniment as if with drums. Odd sort of music; it goes on often now at night . . . Well, it's time to go to bed."

Again he glanced up at the chimney-piece.

"Why, it's quite a little cat," he said.

This rather interested me, for I had said nothing to him about the impression left on my mind that it was bigger than its actual dimensions.

"Just the same size as ever," I said.

"Naturally. But I had been thinking of it as lifesize for some reason," said he.

I went with him to the door, and strolled out with him into the darkness of an overcast night. As we neared his house I saw that big patches of light shone into the road from the windows of the square room next door. Suddenly Hugh laid his hand on my arm.

"There!" he said. "The flutes and drums are at it to-night."

The night was very still, but, listen as I would, I could hear nothing but the rumble of traffic in the street beyond the terrace.

"I can't hear it," I said.

Even as I spoke, I heard it, and the wailing noise whisked me back to Egypt again. The boom of the traffic became for me the beat of the drum, and upon it floated just that squeal and wail of the little reed-pipes which accompany the Arab dances, tuneless and rhythmless, and as old as the temples of the Nile.

"It's like the Arab music that you hear in Egypt," I said.

As we stood listening it ceased to his ears as well as mine, as suddenly as it had begun, and simultaneously the lights in the windows of the square room were extinguished.

We waited a moment in the roadway opposite Hugh's house, but from next door came no sound at all, nor glimmer of illumination from any of its windows . . .

I turned; it was rather chilly to one lately arrived from the south.

"Good night," I said; "we'll meet tomorrow sometime."

I went straight to bed, slept at once, and woke with the impress of a very vivid dream on my mind. There was music in it, familiar Arab music, and there was an immense cat somewhere. Even as I tried to recall it, it faded, and I had but time to recognize it as a hash-up of the happenings of the evening before I went to sleep again.

The normal habits of life quickly reasserted themselves. I had work to do, and there were friends to see; all the minute events of each day stitched themselves into the tapestry of life. But somehow a new thread began to be woven into it, though at the time I did not recognize it as such. It seemed trivial and extraneous that I should so often hear a few staves of that odd music from Naboth's house, or that as often as it fixed my attention it was silent again, as if I had imagined, rather than actually heard it. It was trivial, too, that I should so often see Naboth entering or leaving his house. And then one day I had a sight of him which was unlike any previous experience of mine.

I was standing one morning in the window of my front room. I had idly picked up my lapis lazuli cat, and was holding it in the splash of sunlight that poured in, admiring the texture of its surface which, though it was of hard stone, somehow suggested fur. Then, quite casually, I looked up, and there, a few yards in front of me, leaning on the railings of my garden, and intently observing not me, but what I held, was Naboth. His eyes, fixed on it, blinked in the April sunshine with some purring sensuous content, and Hugh was right on the question of his age; he was neither old nor young, but timeless.

The moment of perception passed; it flashed on and off my mind like the revolving beam of some distant lighthouse. It was just a ray of illumination, and was instantly shut off again, so that it appeared to my conscious mind like some hallucination. He suddenly seemed aware of me, and, turning, walked briskly off down the pavement.

I remember being rather startled, but the effect soon faded, and the incident became to me one of those trivial little things that make a momentary impression and vanish. It was odd, too, but in no way remarkable, that more than once I saw one of those discreet cats of which I have spoken sitting on the little balcony outside my front room, and gravely regarding the interior. I am devoted to cats, and several times I got up in order to open the window and invite it to enter; but each time on my movement it jumped down and slunk away. And April passed into May.

I came back after dining out one night in this month, and found a telephone message from Hugh that I should ring him up on my return. A rather excited voice answered me.

"I thought you would like to know at once," he said. "An hour ago a board was put up on Naboth's house to say that the freehold was for sale. Martin and Smith are the agents. Good night; I'm in bed already."

"You're a true friend," I said.

Early next morning, of course, I presented myself at the house-agent's. The price asked was very moderate, the title perfectly satisfactory. He could give me the keys at once, for the house was empty, and he promised that I could have a couple of days to make up my mind, during which time I was to have the prior right of purchase if I was disposed to pay the full price asked. If, however, I only made an offer, he could not guarantee that the trustees would accept it . . . Hot-foot, with the keys in my pocket, I sped back up the Terrace again.

I found the house completely empty, not of inhabitants only, but of all else. There was not a blind, not a strip of drugget, not a curtain-rod in it from garret to cellar. So much the better, thought I, for there would be no tenants' fixtures to take on. Nor was there any debris of removal, of straw and waste-paper; the house looked as if it was prepared for an occupant instead of just rid of one. All was in apple-pie order, the windows clean, the floors swept, the paint and woodwork bright; it was a clean and polished shell ready for its occupier. My first inspection, of course, was of the big built-out room, which was its chief attraction, and my heart leaped at the sight of its plain spaciousness. On one side was an open fireplace, on the other a coil of pipes for central heating, and at the end, between the windows, a niche let into the wall, as if a statue had once stood there; it might have been designed expressly for my bronze Perseus. The rest of the house presented no particular features; it was on the same plan as my own, and my builder, who inspected it that afternoon, pronounced it to be in excellent condition.

"It looks as if it had been newly done up, and never lived in," he said, "and at the price you mention is a decided bargain."

The same thing struck Hugh when, on his return from his office, I dragged him over to see it.

"Why, it all looks new," he said, "and yet we know that Naboth has been here for years, and was certainly here a week ago. And then there's another thing. When did he remove his furniture? There have been no vans at the house that I have seen."

I was much too pleased at getting my heart's desire to consider anything except that I had got it.

"Oh, I can't bother about little things like that," I said. "Look at my beautiful big room. Piano there, bookcases all along the wall, sofa in front of the fire, Perseus in the niche. Why, it was made for me."

Within the specified two days the house was mine, and within a month papering and distempering, electric fittings, and blinds and curtain-rods were finished, and my move began. Two days were sufficient for the transport of my goods, and at the close of the second my old house was dismantled, except for my bedroom, the contents of which would be moved next day. My servants were installed in the new abode, and that night, after a hurried dinner with Hugh, I went back for a couple more hours' work of hauling and tugging and arranging books in the large room, which it was my purpose to finish first. It was a chilly night for May, and I had had a log-fire lit on the hearth, which from time to time I replenished, in intervals of dusting and arranging. Eventually, when the two hours had lengthened themselves into three, I determined to give over for the present, and, much tired, sat down for a recuperative pause on the edge of my sofa and contemplated with satisfaction the result of my labours. At that moment I was conscious that there was a stale, but aromatic, smell in the room that reminded me of the curious odour that hangs about an Egyptian temple. But I put it down to the dust from my books and the smouldering logs.

The move was completed next day, and after another week I was installed as firmly as if I had been there for years. May slipped by, and June, and my new house never ceased to give me a vivid pleasure; it was always a treat to return to it. Then came a certain afternoon when a strange thing happened.

The day had been wet, but towards evening it cleared up; the pavements soon dried, but the road remained moist and miry. I was close to my house on my way home when I saw form itself on the paving-stones a few yards in front of me the mark of a wet shoe, as if someone invisible to the eye had just

stepped off the road. Another and yet another briskly imprint-
ed themselves, going up towards my house. For the moment I
stood stockstill, and then, with a thumping heart I followed.
The marks of these strange footsteps preceded me right up to
my door; there was one on the very threshold faintly visible.

I let myself in, closing the door, I confess, very quickly
behind me. As I stood there I heard a resounding crash from
my room, which so to speak, startled my fright from me, and
I ran down the little passage and burst in. There, at the far end
of the room was my bronze Perseus fallen from its niche and
lying on the floor. And I knew, by what sixth sense I cannot
tell, that I was not alone in the room and that the presence
there was no human presence.

Now fear is a very odd thing; unless it is overmastering
and overwhelming it always produces its own reaction. Whatever courage we have rises to meet it, and with courage comes
anger that we have given entrance to this unnerving intruder.
That, at any rate, was my case now, and I made an effective
emotional resistance. My servant came running in to see what
the noise was, and we set Perseus on his feet again and examined into the cause of his fall. It was clear enough; a big
piece of plaster had broken away from the niche, and that
must be repaired and strengthened before we reinstated him.
Simultaneously my fear and the sense of an unaccountable
presence in the room slipped from me. The footsteps outside

were still unexplained and I told myself that if I was to shudder at everything I did not understand there would be an end to tranquil existence for ever.

I was dining with Hugh that night; he had been away for the last week, only returning to-day, and he had come in before these slightly agitating events happened to announce his arrival and suggest dinner. I noticed that as he stood chatting for a few minutes, he had once or twice sniffed the air, but he had made no comment, nor had I asked him if he perceived the strange faint odour that every now and then manifested itself to me. I knew it was a great relief to some secretly quaking piece of my mind that he was back, for I was convinced that there was some psychic disturbance going on, either subjectively in my mind, or a real invasion from without. In either case his presence was comforting, not because he is of that stalward breed which believes in nothing beyond the material facts of life, and pooh-poohs these mysterious forces which surround and so strangely interpenetrate existence, but because, while thoroughly believing in them, he has the firm confidence that the deadly and evil powers which occasionally break through into the seeming security of existence are not really to be feared, since they are held in check by forces stronger yet, ready to assist all who realize their protective care. Whether I meant to tell him what had occurred to-day I had not fully determined.

It was not till after dinner that such subjects came up at all, but I had seen there was something on his mind of which he had not spoken yet.

"And your new house," he said at length, "does it still remain as all your fancy painted?"

"I wonder why you ask that," I said.

He gave me a quick glance.

"Mayn't I take any interest in your well-being?" he said.

I knew that something was coming, if I chose to let it.

"I don't think you've ever liked my house from the first," I said. "I believe you think there's something queer about it. I allow that the manner in which I found it empty was odd."

"It was rather," he said. "But so long as it remains empty, except for what you've put in it, it is all right."

I wanted now to press him further.

"What was it you smelt this afternoon in the big room?" I said. "I saw you nosing and sniffing. I have smelt something too. Let's see if we smelt the same thing."

"An odd smell," he said. "Something dusty and stale, but aromatic."

"And what else have you noticed?" I asked.

He paused a moment.

"I think I'll tell you," he said. "This evening from my window I saw you coming up the pavement, and simultaneously I saw, or thought I saw, Naboth cross the road and walk on in front of you. I wondered if you saw him too, for you paused as he stepped on to the pavement in front of you, and then you followed him."

I felt my hands grow suddenly cold, as if the warm current of my blood had been chilled.

"No, I didn't see him," I said, "but I saw his step."

"What do you mean?"

"Just what I say. I saw footprints in front of me, which continued on to my threshold."

"And then?"

"I went in, and a terrific crash startled me. My bronze Perseus had fallen from his niche. And there was something in the room."

There was a scratching noise at the window. Without answering, Hugh jumped up and drew aside the curtain. On the sill was seated a large grey cat, blinking in the light. He advanced to the window, and on his approach the cat jumped down into the garden. The light shone out into the road, and we both saw, standing on the pavement just outside, the figure of a man. He turned and looked at me, and then moved away towards my house next door.

"It's he," said Hugh.

He opened the window and leaned out to see what had become of him. There was no sign of him anywhere, but I saw that light shone from behind the blinds of my room.

"Come on," I said. "Let's see what is happening. Why is my room lit?"

I opened the door of my house with my latchkey, and followed by Hugh went down the short passage to the room. It was perfectly dark, and when I turned the switch, we saw that it was empty. I rang the bell, but no answer came, for it was already late, and doubtless my servants had gone to bed.

"But I saw a strong light from the windows two minutes ago," I said, "and there has been no-one here since."

Hugh was standing by me in the middle of the room. Suddenly he threw out his arm as if striking at something. That thoroughly alarmed me.

"What's the matter?" I asked. "What are you hitting at?"

He shook his head.

"I don't know," he said. "I thought I saw . . . But I'm not sure. But we're in for something if we stop here. Something is coming, though I don't know what."

The light seemed to me to be burning dim; shadows began to collect in the corner of the room, and though outside the night had been clear, the air here was growing thick with a foggy vapour, which smelt dusty and stale and aromatic. Faintly, but getting louder as we waited there in silence, I heard the throb of drums and the wail of flutes. As yet I had no feeling that there were other presences in the place beyond ours, but in the growing dimness I knew that something was coming nearer. Just in front of me was the empty niche from which my bronze had fallen, and looking at it, I saw that something was astir. The shadow within it began to shape itself into a form, and out of it there gleamed two points of greenish light. A moment more and I saw that they were eyes of antique and infinite malignity.

I heard Hugh's voice in a sort of hoarse whisper.

"Look there!" he said. "It's coming! Oh, my God, it's coming!"

Sudden as the lightning that leaps from the heart of the night it came. But it came not with blaze and flash of light, but, as it were, with a stroke of blinding darkness, that fell not on the eye, or on any material sense, but on the spirit, so that I cowered under it in some abandonment of terror. It came from those eyes which gleamed in the niche, and which now I saw to be set in the face of the figure that stood there. The form of it, naked but for a loincloth, was that of a man, the head seemed now human, now to be that of some monstrous cat. And as I looked I knew that if I continued looking there I should be submerged and drowned in that flood of evil that poured from it. As in some catalepsy of nightmare I struggled to tear my eyes from it, but still they were riveted there, gazing on incarnate hate.

Again I heard Hugh's whisper.

"Defy it," he said. "Don't yield an inch."

A swarm of disordered and hellish images were buzzing in my brain, and now I knew as surely as if actual words had been spoken to us that the presence there told me to come to it.

"I've got to go to it," I said. "It's making me go."

I felt his hand tighten on my arm.

"Not a step," he said. "I'm stronger than it is. It will know that soon. Just pray – pray."

Suddenly his arm shot out in front of me, pointing at the presence.

"By the power of God!" he shouted. "By the power of God!"

There was dead silence. The light of those eyes faded, and then came dawn on the darkness of the room. It was quiet and orderly, the niche was empty, and there on the sofa by me was Hugh, his face white and streaming with sweat.

"It's over," he said, and without pause fell fast asleep.

Now we have often talked over together what happened that evening. Of what seemed to happen I have already given the account, which anyone may believe or not, precisely as they please. He, as I, was conscious of a presence wholly evil, and he tells me that all the time that those eyes gleamed from the niche, he was trying to realize what he believed, namely, that only one power in the world is Omnipotent, and that the moment he gained that realization the presence collapsed.

What exactly that presence was it is impossible to say. It looks as if it was the essence or spirit of one of those mysterious Egyptian cults, of which the force survived, and was seen and felt in this quiet Terrace. That it was embodied in Naboth seems (among all these incredibilities) possible, and Naboth certainly has never been seen again. Whether or not it was connected with the worship and cult of cats might occur to the mythological mind, and it is perhaps worthy of record that I found next morning my little lapis lazuli image, which stood on the chimney-piece, broken into fragments. It was too badly damaged to mend, and I am not sure that, in any case, I should have attempted to have it restored.

Finally, there is no more tranquil and pleasant room in London than the one built out in front of my house in Bagnell Terrace.

MONKEYS

Dr Hugh Morris, while still in the early thirties of his age, had justly earned for himself the reputation of being one of the most dexterous and daring surgeons in his profession, and both in his private practice and in his voluntary work at one of the great London hospitals his record of success as an operator was unparalleled among his colleagues. He believed that vivisection was the most fruitful means of progress in the science of surgery, holding, rightly or wrongly, that he was justified in causing suffering to animals, though sparing them all possible pain, if thereby he could reasonably hope to gain fresh knowledge about similar operations on human beings which would save life or mitigate suffering; the motive was good, and the gain already immense. But he had nothing but scorn for those who, for their own amusement, took out packs of hounds to run foxes to death, or matched two greyhounds to see which would give the death-grip to a single terrified hare: that, to him, was wanton torture, utterly unjustifiable. Year in and year out, he took no holiday at all, and for the most part he occupied his leisure, when the day's work was over, in study.

He and his friend Jack Madden were dining together one

warm October night at his house looking on to Regent's Park. The windows of his drawing-room on the ground-floor were open, and they sat smoking, when dinner was done, on the broad window-seat. Madden was starting next day for Egypt, where he was engaged in archæological work, and he would be engaged throughout the winter in the excavation of a newly-discovered cemetery across the river from Luxor, near Medinet Habu. But it was no good.

'When my eye begins to fail and my fingers to falter,' said Morris, 'it will be time for me to think of taking my ease. What do I want with a holiday? I should be pining to get back to my work all the time. I like work better than loafing. Purely selfish.'

'Well, be unselfish for once,' said Madden. 'Besides, your work would benefit. It can't be good for a man never to relax. Surely freshness is worth something.'

'Precious little if you're as strong as I am. I believe in continual concentration if one wants to make progress. One may be tired, but why not? I'm not tired when I'm actually engaged on a dangerous operation, which is what matters. And time's so short. Twenty years from now I shall be past my best, and I'll have my holiday then, and when my holiday is over, I shall fold my hands and go to sleep for ever and ever. Thank God, I've got no fear that there's an after-life. The spark of vitality that has animated us burns low and then goes out like a windblown candle, and as for my body, what do I care what happens to that when I have done with it? Nothing will survive of me except some small contribution I may have made to surgery, and in a few years' time that will be superseded. But for that I perish utterly.'

Madden squirted some soda into his glass.

'Well, if you've quite settled that –' he began.

'I haven't settled it, science has,' said Morris. 'The body is transmuted into other forms, worms batten on it, it helps to feed the grass, and some animal consumes the grass. But as for the survival of the individual spirit of a man, show me one title of scientific evidence to support it. Besides, if it did survive, all the evil and malice in it must surely survive too. Why should the death of the body purge that away? It's a nightmare to contemplate such a thing, and oddly enough, unhinged people like spiritualists want to persuade us for our consolation that the nightmare is true. But odder still are those old Egyptians of yours, who thought that there was something sacred about their bodies, after they were quit of them. And didn't you tell me that they covered their coffins with curses on anyone who disturbed their bones?'

'Constantly,' said Madden. 'It's the general rule in fact. Marrowy curses written in hieroglyphics on the mummy-case or carved on the sarcophagus.'

'But that's not going to deter you this winter from opening as many tombs as you can find, and rifling from them any objects of interest or value.'

Madden laughed.

'Certainly it isn't,' he said. 'I take out of the tombs all objects of art, and I unwind the mummies to find and annex their scarabs and jewellery. But I make an absolute rule always to bury the bodies again. I don't say that I believe in the power of those curses, but anyhow a mummy in a museum is an indecent object.'

'But if you found some mummied body with an interesting malformation, wouldn't you send it to some anatomical institute?' asked Morris.

'It has never happened to me yet,' said Madden, 'but I'm pretty sure I shouldn't.'

'Then you're a superstitious Goth and an anti-educational Vandal,' remarked Morris . . . 'Hullo, what's that?' He leant out of the window as he spoke. The light from the room vividly illuminated the square of lawn outside, and across it was crawling the small twitching shape of some animal. Hugh Morris vaulted out of the window, and presently returned, carrying carefully in his spread hands a little grey monkey, evidently desperately injured. Its hind legs were stiff and outstretched as if it was partially paralysed.

Morris ran his soft deft fingers over it.

'What's the matter with the little beggar, I wonder,' he

said. 'Paralysis of the lower limbs: it looks like some lesion of the spine.'

The monkey lay quite still, looking at him with anguished appealing eyes as he continued his manipulation.

'Yes, I thought so,' he said. 'Fracture of one of the lumbar vertebræ. What luck for me! It's a rare injury, but I've often wondered. . . . And perhaps luck for the monkey too, though that's not very probable. If he was a man and a patient of mine, I shouldn't dare to take the risk. But, as it is . . .'

Jack Madden started on his southward journey next day, and by the middle of November was at work on this newly-discovered cemetery. He and another Englishman were in charge of the excavation, under the control of the Antiquity Department of the Egyptian Government. In order to be close to their work and to avoid the daily ferrying across the Nile from Luxor, they hired a bare roomy native house in the adjoining village of Gurnah. A reef of low sandstone cliff ran northwards from here towards the temple and terraces of Deir-el-Bahari, and it was in the face of this and on the level below it that the ancient graveyard lay. There was much accumulation of sand to be cleared away before the actual exploration of the tombs could begin, but trenches cut below the foot of the sandstone ridge showed that there was an extensive area to investigate.

The more important sepulchres, they found, were hewn in the face of this small cliff: many of these had been rifled in ancient days, for the slabs forming the entrances into them had been split, and the mummies unwound, but now and then Madden unearthed some tomb that had escaped these marauders, and in one he found the sarcophagus of a priest of the nineteenth dynasty, and that alone repaid weeks of fruitless work. There were nearly a hundred *ushaptiu* figures of the finest blue glaze; there were four alabaster vessels in which had been placed the viscera of the dead man removed before embalming: there was a table of which the top was inlaid with squares of variously coloured glass, and the legs were of carved ivory and ebony: there were the priest's sandals adorned with exquisite silver filagree: there was his staff of office inlaid with a diaper-pattern of cornelian and gold, and on the head of it, forming the handle, was the figure of a squatting cat, carved in amethyst, and the mummy, when unwound, was found to be decked with a necklace of gold plaques and onyx beads. All these were sent down to the Gizeh Museum at Cairo, and Madden reinterred the mummy at the foot of the cliff below the tomb. He wrote to Hugh Morris describing this find, and laying stress on the unbroken splendour of these crystalline winter days, when from morning to night the sun cruised across the blue, and on the cool nights when the stars rose and set on the vapourless rim of the desert. If by chance Hugh should change his mind, there was ample room for him in this house at Gurnah, and he would be very welcome.

A fortnight later Madden received a telegram from his friend. It stated that he had been unwell and was starting at once by long sea to Port Said, and would come straight up to Luxor. In due course he announced his arrival at Cairo and Madden went across the river next day to meet him: it was reassuring to find him as vital and active as ever, the picture of bronzed health. The two were alone that night, for Madden's colleague had gone for a week's trip up the Nile, and they sat out, when dinner was done, in the enclosed courtyard adjoining the house. Till then Madden had shied off the subject of himself and his health.

'Now I may as well tell you what's been amiss with me,' he said, 'for I know I look a fearful fraud as an invalid, and physically I've never been better in my life. Every organ has been functioning perfectly except one, but something suddenly went wrong there just once. It was like this.'

He paused a moment.

'After you left,' he said, 'I went on as usual for another month or so, very busy, very serene and, I may say, very successful. Then one morning I arrived at the hospital when there was one perfectly ordinary but major operation waiting for me. The patient, a man, was wheeled into the theatre anæsthetized, and I was just about to make the first incision into the abdomen, when I saw that there was sitting on his chest a little grey monkey. It was not looking at me, but at the fold of skin which I held between my thumb and finger. I knew, of course, that there was no monkey there, and that what I saw was a hallucination, and I think you'll agree that there was nothing much wrong with my nerves when I tell you that I went through the operation with clear eyes and an unshaking hand. I had to go on: there was no choice about the matter. I couldn't say: "Please take that monkey away," for I knew there was no monkey there. Nor could I say: "Somebody else must do this, as I have a distressing hallucination that there is a monkey sitting on the patient's chest." There would have been an end of me as a surgeon and no mistake. All the time I was at work it sat there absorbed in the most part in what I was doing and peering into the wound, but now and then it looked up at me, and chattered with rage. Once it fingered a spring-forceps which clipped a severed vein, and that was the worst moment of all . . . At the end it was carried out still balancing itself on the man's chest . . . I think I'll have a drink. Strongish, please . . . Thanks.'

'A beastly experience,' he said when he had drunk. 'Then I went straight away from the hospital to consult my old friend Robert Angus, the alienist and nerve-specialist, and told him exactly what had happened to me. He made several tests, he examined my eyes, tried my reflexes, took my bood-pressure: there was nothing wrong with any of them. Then he asked me questions about my general health and manner of life, and among these questions was one which I am sure has already occurred to you, namely, had anything occurred to me lately, or even remotely, which was likely to make me visualize a monkey. I told him that a few weeks ago a monkey with a broken lumbar vertebra had crawled on to my lawn, and that I had attempted an operation – binding the broken vertebra with wire – which had occurred to me before as a possibility. You remember the night, no doubt?'

'Perfectly,' said Madden, 'I started for Egypt next day. What happened to the monkey, by the way?'

'It lived for two days: I was pleased, because I had expected it would die under the anæsthetic, or immediately afterwards from shock. To get back to what I was telling you. When Angus had asked all his questions, he gave me a good wigging. He said that I had persistently overtaxed my brain for years, without giving it any rest or change of occupation, and that if I wanted to be of any further use in the world, I must drop my work at once for a couple of months. He told me that my brain was tired out and that I had persisted in stimulating it. A man like me, he said, was no better than a confirmed drunkard, and that, as a warning, I had had a touch of an appropriate delirium tremens. The cure was to drop work, just as a drunkard must drop drink. He laid it on hot and strong: he said I was on the verge of a breakdown, entirely owing to my own foolishness, but that I had wonderful physical health, and that if I did break down I should be a disgrace. Above all – and this seemed to me awfully sound advice – he told me not to attempt to avoid thinking about what had happened to me. If I kept my mind mind off it, I should be perhaps driving it into the subconscious, and then there might be bad trouble. "Rub it in: think what a fool you've been," he said. "Face it, dwell on it, make yourself thoroughly ashamed of yourself." Monkeys, too: I wasn't to avoid the thought of monkeys. In fact, he recommended me to go straight away to the Zoological Gardens, and spend an hour in the monkey-house.'

'Odd treatment,' interrupted Madden.

'Brilliant treatment. My brain, he explained, had rebelled against its slavery, and had hoisted a red flag with the device of a monkey on it. I must show it that I wasn't frightened at its bogus monkeys. I must retort on it by making myself look at dozens of real ones which could bite and maul you savagely, instead of one little sham monkey that had no existence at all. At the same time I must take the red flag seriously, recognize there was danger, and rest. And he promised me that sham monkeys wouldn't trouble me again. Are there any real ones in Egypt, by the way?'

'Not so far as I know,' said Madden. 'But there must have been once, for there are many images of them in tombs and temples.'

'That's good. We'll keep their memory green and my brain

cool. Well, there's my story. What do you think of it?'

'Terrifying,' said Madden. 'But you must have got nerves of iron to get through that operation with the monkey watching.'

'A hellish hour. Out of some disordered slime in my brain there had crawled this unbidden thing, which showed itself, apparently substantial, to my eyes. It didn't come from outside: my eyes hadn't told my brain that there was a monkey sitting on the man's chest, but my brain had told my eyes so, making fools of them. I felt as if someone whom I absolutely trusted had played me false. Then again I have wondered whether some instinct in my subconscious mind revolted against vivisection. My reason says that it is justified, for it teaches us how pain can be relieved and death postponed for human beings. But what if my subconscious persuaded my brain to give me a good fright, and reproduce before my eyes the semblance of a monkey, just when I was putting into practice what I had learned from dealing out pain and death to animals?'

He got up suddenly.

'What about bed?' he said. 'Five hours' sleep was enough for me when I was at work, but now I believe I could sleep the clock round every night.'

Young Wilson, Madden's colleague in the excavations, returned next day and the work went steadily on. One of them was on the spot to start it soon after sunrise, and either one or both of them were superintending it, with an interval of a couple of hours at noon, until sunset. When the mere work of clearing the face of the sandstone cliff was in progress and of carting away the silted soil, the presence of one of them sufficed, for there was nothing to do but to see that the workmen shovelled industriously, and passed regularly with their baskets of earth and sand on their shoulders to the dumping-grounds, which stretched away from the area to be excavated, in lengthening peninsulas of trodden soil. But, as they advanced along the sandstone ridge, there would now and then appear a chiselled smoothness in the cliff and then both must be alert. There was great excitement to see if, when they exposed the hewn slab that formed the door into the tomb, it had escaped ancient marauders, and still stood in place and intact for the modern to explore. But now for many days they came upon no sepulchre that had not already been opened. The mummy, in these cases, had been unwound in the search for necklaces and scarabs, and its scattered bones lay about. Madden was always at pains to reinter these.

At first Hugh Morris was assiduous in watching the excavations, but as day after day went by without anything of interest turning up, his attendance grew less frequent: it was too much of a holiday to watch the day-long removal of sand from one place to another. He visited the Tomb of the Kings, he went across the river and saw the temples at Karnak, but his appetite for antiquities was small. On other days he rode in the desert, or spent the day with friends at one of the Luxor hotels. He came home from there one evening in rare good spirits, for he had played lawn-tennis with a woman on whom he had operated for malignant tumour six months before and she had skipped about the court like a two-year-old. 'God, how I want to be at work again,' he exclaimed. 'I wonder whether I ought not to have stuck it out, and defied my brain to frighten me with bogies.'

The weeks passed on, and now there were but two days left before his return to England, where he hoped to resume work at once: his tickets were taken and his berth booked. As he sat over breakfast that morning with Wilson, there came a workman from the excavation, with a note scribbled in hot haste by Madden, to say that they had just come upon a tomb which seemed to be unrifled, for the slab that closed it was in place and unbroken. To Wilson, the news was like the sight of a sail to a marooned mariner, and when, a quarter of an hour later, Morris followed him, he was just in time to see the slab prised away. There was no sarcophagus within, for the rock walls did duty for that, but there lay there, varnished and bright in hue as if painted yesterday, the mummycase roughly following the outline of the human form. By it stood the alabaster vases containing the entrails of the dead, and at each corner of the sepulchre there were carved out of the sandstone rock, forming, as it were, pillars to support the roof, thick-set images of squatting apes. The mummy-case was hoisted out and carried away by workmen on a bier of boards into the courtyard of the excavators' house at Gurnah, for the opening of it and the unwrapping of the dead.

They got to work that evening directly they had fed: the face painted on the lid was that of a girl or young woman, and presently deciphering the hieroglyphic inscription, Madden read out that within lay the body of A-pen-ara, daughter of the overseer of the cattle of Senmut.

'Then follow the usual formulas,' he said. 'Yes, yes . . . ah, you'll be interested in this, Hugh, for you asked me once about it. A-pen-ara curses any who desecrates or meddles with her bones, and should anyone do so, the guardians of her sepulchre will see to him, and he shall die childless and in panic and agony; also the guardian of her sepulchre will tear the hair from his head and scoop his eyes from their sockets, and pluck the thumbs from his right hand, as a man plucks the young blade of corn from its sheath.'

Morris laughed.

'Very pretty little attentions,' he said. 'And who are the guardians of this sweet young lady's sepulchre? Those four great apes carved at the corners?'

'No doubt. But we won't trouble them, for to-morrow I shall bury Miss A-pen-ara's bones again with all decency in the trench at the foot of her tomb. They'll be safer there, for if we put them back where we found them, there would be pieces of her hawked about by half the donkey-boys in Luxor in a few days. "Buy a mummy hand, lady? . . . Foot of a Gyppy Queen, only ten piastres, gentlemen" . . . Now for the unwinding.'

It was dark by now, and Wilson fetched out a paraffin lamp, which burned unwaveringly in the still air. The lid of the mummy-case was easily detached, and within was the slim, swaddled body. The embalming had not been very thoroughly done, for all the skin and flesh had perished from the head, leaving only bones of the skull stained brown with bitumen. Round it was a mop of hair, which with the ingress of the air subsided like a belated *soufflé*, and crumbled into dust. The cloth that swathes the body was as brittle, but round the neck, still just holding together, was a collar of curious and rare workmanship: little ivory figures of squatting apes alternated with silver beads. But again a touch broke the thread that strung them together, and each had to be picked out singly. A bracelet of scarabs and cornelians still clasped one of the fleshless wrists, and then they turned the body over in order to get at the members of the necklace which lay beneath the nape. The rotted mummy-cloth fell away altogether from the back, disclosing the shoulder-blades and the spine down as far as the pelvis. Here the embalming had been better done, for the bones still held together with remnants of muscle and cartilage.

Hugh Morris suddenly sprang to his feet.

'My God, look there!' he cried, 'one of the lumbar vertebræ, there at the base of the spine, has been broken and clamped together with a metal band. To hell with your antiquities: let me come and examine something much more modern than any of us!'

He pushed Jack Madden aside, and peered at this marvel of surgery.

'Put the lamp closer,' he said, as if directing some nurse at an operation. 'Yes: that vertebra has been broken right across and has been clamped together. No one has ever, as far as I know, attempted such an operation except myself, and I have only performed it on that little paralysed monkey that crept into my garden one night. But some Egyptian surgeon, more than three thousand years ago, performed it on a woman. And look, look! She lived afterwards, for the broken vertebra put out that bony efflorescence of healing which has encroached over the metal band. That's a slow process, and it must have taken place during her lifetime, for there is no such energy in a corpse. The woman lived long: probably she recovered completely. And my wretched little monkey only lived two days and was dying all the time.'

Those questing hawk-visioned fingers of the surgeon perceived more finely than actual sight, and now he closed his eyes as the tip of them felt their way about the fracture in the broken vertebra and the clamping metal band.

'The band doesn't encircle the bone,' he said, 'and there are no studs attaching it. There must have been a spring in it, which, when it was clasped there, kept it tight. It has been clamped round the bone itself: the surgeon must have scraped the verebra clean of flesh before he attached it. I would give two years of my life to have looked on, like a student, at that masterpiece of skill, and it was worth while giving up two months of my work only to have seen the result. And the injury itself is so rare, this breaking of a spinal vertebra. To be sure, the hangman does something of the sort, but there's no mending that! Good Lord, my holiday has not been a waste of time!'

Madden settled that it was not worth while to send the mummy-case to the museum at Gizeh, for it was of a very ordinary type, and when the examination was over they lifted the body back into it, for reinterment next day. It was now long after midnight and presently the house was dark.

Hugh Morris slept on the ground-floor in a room adjoining the yard where the mummy-case lay. He remained long awake marvelling at that astonishing piece of surgical skill performed, according to Madden, some thirty-five centuries ago. So occupied had his mind been with homage that not till now did he realize that the tangible proof and witness of the operation would to-morrow be buried again and lost to science. He must persuade Madden to let him detach at least three of the vertebræ, the mended one and those immediately above and below it, and take them back to England as demonstration of what could be done: he would lecture on his exhibit and present it to the Royal College of Surgeons for example and incitement. Other trained eyes beside his own must see what had been successfully achieved by some unknown operator in the nineteenth dynasty . . . But supposing Madden refused? He always made a point of scrupulously reburying these remains: it was a principle with him, and no doubt some superstition-complex – the hardest of all to combat with because of its sheer unreasonableness – was involved. Briefly, it was impossible to risk the chance of his refusal.

He got out of bed, listened for a moment by his door, and then softly went out into the yard. The moon had risen, for the brightness of the stars was paled, and though no direct rays shone into the walled enclosure, the dusk was dispersed by the toneless luminosity of the sky, and he had no need of a lamp. He drew the lid off the coffin, and folded back the tattered cerements which Madden had replaced over the body. He had thought that those lower vertebræ of which he was determined to possess himself would be easily detached, so far perished were the muscle and cartilage which held them together, but they cohered as if they had been clamped, and it required the utmost force of his powerful fingers to snap the spine, and as he did so the severed bones cracked as with the noise of a pistol-shot. But there was no sign that anyone in the house had heard it, there came no sound of steps, nor lights in the windows. One more fracture was needed, and then the relic was his. Before he replaced the ragged cloths he looked again at the stained fleshless bones. Shadow dwelt in the empty eye-sockets, as if black sunken eyes still lay there, fixedly regarding him, the lipless mouth snarled and grimaced. Even as he looked some change came over its aspect, and for one brief moment he fancied that there lay staring up at him the face of a great brown ape. But instantly that illusion vanished, and replacing the lid he went back to his room.

The mummy-case was reinterred next day, and two evenings after Morris left Luxor by the night train for Cairo, to join a homeward-bound P & O at Port Said. There were some hours to spare before his ship sailed, and having deposited his luggage, including a locked leather despatch-case, on board, he lunched at the Café Tewfik near the quay. There was a garden in front of it with palm trees and trellises gaily clad in bougainvillias: a low wooden rail separated it from the street, and Morris had a table close to this. As he ate he watched the polychromatic pageant of Eastern life passing by: there were Egyptian officials in broad-cloth frock coats and red fezzes; barefooted splay-toed fellahin in blue gabardines; veiled women in white making stealthy eyes at passers-by; half-naked gutter-snipes, one with a sprig of scarlet hibiscus behind his ear; travellers from India with solar topees and an air of aloof British superiority; dishevelled sons of the Prophet in green turbans; a stately sheik in a white *burnous*; French painted ladies of a professional class with lace-rimmed parasols and provocative glances; a wild-eyed dervish in an accordion-pleated skirt, chewing betel-nut and slightly foaming at the mouth. A Greek boot-black with box adorned with brass plaques tapped his brushes on it to encourage customers, an Egyptian girl squatted in the gutter beside a gramophone, steamers passing into the Canal hooted on their syrens.

Then at the edge of the pavement there sauntered by a young Italian harnessed to a barrel-organ: with one hand he ground out a popular air by Verdi, in the other he held out a tin can for the tributes of music-lovers: a small monkey in a yellow jacket, tethered to his wrist, sat on the top of his instrument. The musician had come opposite the table where Morris sat: Morris liked the gay tinkling tune, and feeling in his pocket for a piastre, he beckoned to him. The boy grinned and stepped up to the rail.

Then suddenly the melancholy-eyed monkey leaped from its place on the organ and sprang on to the table by which Morris sat. It alighted there, chattering with rage in a crash of broken glass. A flower-vase was upset, a plate clattered on to the floor. Morris's coffee-cup discharged its black contents on the tablecloth. Next moment the Italian had twitched the frenzied little beast back to him, and it fell head downwards on the pavement. A shrill hubbub arose, the waiter at Morris's table hurried up with voluble execrations, a policeman kicked out at the monkey as it lay on the ground, the barrel-organ tottered and crashed on the roadway. Then all subsided again, and the Italian boy picked up the little body from the pavement. He held it out in his hands to Morris.

'*E morto*,' he said.

'Serves it right, too,' retorted Morris. 'Why did it fly at me like that?'

He travelled back to London by long sea, and day after day that tragic little incident, in which he had had no responsible part, began to make a sort of colouring matter in his mind during those hours of lazy leisure on ship-board, when a man gives about an equal inattention to the book he reads and to what passes round him. Sometimes if the shadow of a seagull overhead slid across the deck towards him, there leaped into his brain, before his eyes could reassure him, the ludicrous fancy that this shadow was a monkey springing at him. One day they ran into a gale from the west: there was a crash of glass at his elbow as a sudden lurch of the ship upset a laden steward, and Morris jumped from his seat thinking that a monkey had leaped on to his table again. There was a cinematograph show in the saloon one evening, in which some naturalist exhibited the films he had taken of wild life in Indian jungles: when he put on the screen the picture of a company of monkeys swinging their way through the trees Morris involuntarily clutched the sides of his chair in hideous panic that lasted but a fraction of a second, until he recalled to himself that he was only looking at a film in the saloon of a steamer passing up the coast of Portugal. He came sleepy into his cabin one night and saw some animal crouching by the locked leather despatch-case. His breath caught in his throat before he perceived that this was a friendly cat which rose with gleaming eyes and arched its back . . .

These fantastic unreasonable alarms were disquieting. He had as yet no repetition of the hallucination that he saw a monkey, but some deep-buried 'idea,' to cure which he had taken two months' holiday, was still unpurged from his mind. He must consult Robert Angus again when he got home, and seek further advice. Probably that incident at Port Said had rekindled the obscure trouble, and there was this added to it, that he knew he was now frightened of real monkeys: there was terror sprouting in the dark of his soul. But as for it having any connection with his pilfered treasure, so rank and childish a superstition deserved only the ridicule he gave it. Often he unlocked his leather case and sat poring over that miracle of surgery which made practical again long-forgotten dexterities.

But it was good to be back in England. For the last three days of the voyage no menace had flashed out on him from the unknown dusks, and surely he had been disquieting himself in vain. There was a light mist lying over Regent's Park on this warm March evening, and a drizzle of rain was falling. He made an appointment for the next morning with the specialist, he telephoned to the hospital that he had returned and hoped to resume work at once. He dined in very good spirits, talking to his manservant, and, as subsequently came out, he showed him his treasured bones, telling him that he had taken the relic from a mummy which he had seen unwrapped and that he meant to lecture on it. When he went up to bed he carried the leather case with him. Bed was comfortable after the ship's berth, and through his open window came the soft hissing of the rain on to the shrubs outside.

His servant slept in the room immediately over his. A little before dawn he woke with a start, roused by horrible cries from somewhere close at hand. Then came words yelled out in a voice that he knew:

'Help! Help!' it cried. 'O my God, my God! Ah – h –' and it rose to a scream again.

The man hurried down and clicked on the light in his master's room as he entered. The cries had ceased: only a low moaning came from the bed. A huge ape with busy hands was bending over it; then taking up the body that lay there by the neck and the hips he bent it backwards and it cracked like a dry stick. Then it tore open the leather case that was on a table by the bedside, and with something that gleamed white in its dripping fingers it shambled to the window and disappeared.

A doctor arrived within half an hour, but too late. Handfuls of hair with flaps of skin attached had been torn from the head of the murdered man, both eyes were scooped out of their sockets, the right thumb had been plucked off the hand, and the back was broken across the lower vertebræ.

Nothing has since come to light which could rationally explain the tragedy. No large ape had escaped from the neighbouring Zoological Gardens, or, as far as could be ascertained, from elsewhere, nor was the monstrous visitor of that night ever seen again. Morris's servant had only had the briefest sight of it, and his description of it at the inquest did not tally with that of any known simian type. And the sequel was even more mysterious, for Madden, returing to England at the close of the season in Egypt, had asked Morris's servant exactly what it was that his master had shown him the evening before as having been taken by him from a mummy which he had seen unwrapped, and had got from him a sufficiently conclusive account of it. Next autumn he continued his excavations in the cemetery at Gurnah, and he disinterred once more the mummy-case of A-pen-ara and opened it. But the spinal vertebræ were all in place and complete: one had round it the silver clip which Morris had hailed as a unique achievement in surgery.

GAVON'S EVE

It is only the largest kind of ordnance map that records the existence of the village of Gavon, in the shire of Sutherland, and it is perhaps surprising that any map on whatever scale should mark so small and huddled a group of huts, set on a bare, bleak headland between moor and sea, and, so one would have thought, of no import at all to any who did not happen to live there. But the river Gavon, on the right bank of which stands this half-dozen chimney-less and wind-swept habitations, is a geographical fact of far greater interest to outsiders, for the salmon there are heavy fish, the mouth of the river is clear of nets, and all the way up to Gavon Loch, some six miles inland, the coffee-coloured water lies in pool after deep pool, which verge, if the river is in order and the angler moderately sanguine, on a fishing probability amounting almost to a certainty. In any case during the first fortnight of September last I had no blank day on those delectable waters, and up till the 15th of that month there was no day on which some one at the lodge in which I was stopping did not land a fish out of the famous Pict's pool. But after the 15th that pool was not fished again. The reason why is here set forward.

The river at this point, after some hundred yards of rapid, makes a sudden turn round a rocky angle, and plunges madly into the pool itself. Very deep water lies at the head of it, but deeper still further down on the east side, where a portion of the stream flicks back again in a swift dark backwater towards the top of the pool again. It is fishable only from the western bank, for to the east, above this backwater, a great wall of black and basaltic rock, heaved up no doubt by some fault in strata, rises sheer from the river to the height of some 60 feet. It is in fact nearly precipitous on both sides, heavily serrated at the top, and of so curious a thinness, that at about the middle of it where a fissure breaks its topmost edge, and some twenty feet from the top, there exists a long hole, a sort of lancet window, one would say, right through the rock, so that a slit of daylight can be seen through it. Since, therefore, no one would care to cast his line standing perched on that razor-edged eminence, the pool must needs be fished from the western bank. A decent fly, however, will cover it all.

It is on the western bank that there stand the remains of that which give its title to the pool, namely, the ruins of a Pict castle, built out of rough and scarcely hewn masonry, unmortared but on a certain large and impressive scale, and in a very well-preserved condition considering its extreme antiquity. It is circular in shape and measures some twenty yards of diameter in its internal span. A staircase of large blocks with a rise of at least a foot leads up to the main gate, and opposite this on the side towards the river is another smaller postern through which down a rather hazardously steep slope a scrambling path, where progress demands both caution and activity, conducts to the head of the pool which lies immediately beneath it. A gate-chamber still roofed over exists in the solid wall: inside there are foundation indications of three rooms, and in the centre of all a very deep hole, probably a well. Finally, just outside the postern leading to the river is a small artificially levelled platform some twenty feet across, as if made to support some super-incumbent edifice. Certain stone slabs and blocks are dispersed over it.

Brora, the post-town of Gavon, lies some six miles to the south-west, and from it a track over the moor leads to the rapids immediately above the Picts' pool, across which by somewhat extravagant striding from boulder to boulder a man can pass dry-foot when the river is low, and make his way up a steep path to the north of the basaltic rock, and so to the village. But this transit demands a steady head, and at the best is a somewhat giddy passage. Otherwise the road between it and Brora lies in a long detour higher up the moor, passing by the gates of Gavon Lodge, where I was stopping. For some vague and ill-defined reason the pool itself and the Picts' Castle had an uneasy reputation on the countryside, and several times trudging back from a day's fishing I have known my gillie take a longish circuit, though heavy with fish, rather than make this short cut in the dusk by the castle. On the first occasion when Sandy, a strapping yellow-bearded viking of twenty-five, did this he gave as a reason that the ground round about the castle was 'mossy', though as a God-fearing man, he must have known he lied. But on another occasion he was more frank, and said that the Picts' pool was 'no canny' after sunset. I am now inclined to agree with him, though, when he lied about it, I think it was because as a God-fearing man he feared the devil also.

It was on the evening of September 14 that I was walking back with my host, Hugh Graham, from the forest beyond the lodge. It had been a day unseasonably hot for the time of year, and the hills were blanketed with soft, furry clouds. Sandy, the gillie of whom I have spoken, was behind with the ponies, and, idly enough, I told Hugh about his strange distaste for the Picts' pool after sunset. He listened, frowning a little.

'That's curious,' he said. 'I know there is some dim local superstition about the place, but last year certainly Sandy used to laugh at it. I remember asking him what ailed the place, and he said he thought nothing about the rubbish the folk talked. But this year you say he avoids it.'

'On several occasions with me he has done so.'

Hugh smoked a while in silence, striding noiselessly over the dusky fragrant heather.

'Poor chap,' he said, 'I don't know what to do about him. He's becoming useless.'

'Drink?' I asked.

'Yes, drink in a secondary manner. But trouble led to drink, and trouble, I am afraid, is leading him to worse than drink.'

'The only thing worse than drink is the devil,' I remarked.

'Precisely. That's where he is going. He goes there often.'

'What on earth do you mean?' I asked.

'Well, it's rather curious,' said Hugh. 'You know I dabble a bit in folklore and local superstition, and I believe I am on the track of something odder than odd. Just wait a moment.'

We stood there in the gathering dusk till the ponies laboured up the hillside to us, Sandy with his six feet of lithe strength strolling easily beside them up the steep brae, as if his long day's trudging had but served to half awaken his dormant powers of limb.

'Going to see Mistress Macpherson again tonight?' asked Hugh.

'Aye, puir body,' said Sandy. 'She's auld, and she's lone.'

'Very kind of you, Sandy,' said Hugh, and we walked on.

'What then?' I asked when the ponies had fallen behind again.

'Why, superstition lingers here,' said Hugh, 'and it's supposed she's a witch. To be quite candid with you, the thing interests me a good deal. Supposing you asked me, on oath, whether I believed in witches, I should say "No". But if you asked me again, on oath, whether I suspected I believed in them, I should, I think, say "Yes". And the fifteenth of this month – tomorrow – is Gavon's Eve.'

'And what in Heaven's name is that?' I asked. 'And who is Gavon? And what's the trouble?'

'Well, Gavon is the person, I suppose, not saint, who is what we should call the eponymous hero of this district. And the trouble is Sandy's trouble. Rather a long story. But there's a long mile in front of us yet, if you care to be told.'

During that mile I heard. Sandy had been engaged a year ago to a girl of Gavon who was in service at Inverness. In March last he had gone, without giving notice, to see her, and as he walked up the street in which her mistress' house stood, had met her suddenly face to face, in company with a man whose clipped speech betrayed him English, whose manner a kind of gentleman. He had a flourish of his hat for Sandy, pleasure to see him, and scarcely any need of explanation as to how he came to be walking with Catrine. It was the most natural thing possible, for a city like Inverness boasted its innocent urbanities, and a girl could stroll with a man. And for the time, since also Catrine was so frankly pleased to see him, Sandy was satisfied. But after his return to Gavon, suspicion, fungus-like, grew rank in his mind, with the result that a month ago he had, with infinite pains and blottings, written a letter to Catrine, urging her return and immediate marriage. Thereafter it was known that she left Inverness; it was known that she had arrived by train at Brora. From Brora she had started to walk across the moor by the path leading just above the Picts' Castle, crossing the rapids to Gavon, leaving her box to be sent by the carrier. But at Gavon she had never arrived. Also it was said, that although it was a hot afternoon, she wore a big cloak.

By this time we had come to the lodge, the lights of which showed dim and blurred through the thick hill-mists that had streamed sullenly down from the higher ground.

'And the rest,' said Hugh, 'which is as fantastic as this is sober fact, I will tell you later.'

Now, a fruit-bearing determination to go to bed is, to my mind, as difficult to ripen as a fruit-bearing determination to get up, and in spite of our long day, I was glad when Hugh (the rest of the men having yawned themselves out of the smoking-room) came back from the hospitable dispensing of bedroom candlesticks with a briskness that denoted that, as far as he was concerned, the distressing determination was not imminent.

'As regards Sandy,' I suggested.

'Ah, I also was thinking of that,' he said. 'Well, Catrine

Gordon left Brora, and never arrived here. That is fact. Now for what remains. Have you any remembrance of a woman always alone walking about the moor by the loch? I think I once called your attention to her.'

'Yes, I remember,' I said. 'Not Catrine, surely; a very old woman, awful to look at. Moustache, whiskers, and muttering to herself. Always looking at the ground, too.'

'Yes, that is she – not Catrine. Catrine! My word, a May morning! But the other – it is Mrs. Macpherson, reputed witch. Well, Sandy trudges there, a mile and more away, every night to see her. You know Sandy: Adonis of the north. Now, can you account by any natural explanation for that fact? That he goes off after a long day to see an old hag in the hills?'

'It would seem unlikely,' said I.

'Unlikely! Well, yes, unlikely.'

Hugh got up from his chair and crossed the room to where a bookcase of rather fusty-looking volumes stood between windows. He took a small morocco-bound book from a top shelf.

'Superstitions of Sutherlandshire,' he said, as he handed it to me. 'Turn to page 128, and read.'

I obeyed, and read:

'September 15 appears to have been the date of what we may call this devil festival. On the night of that day the powers of darkness held pre-eminent dominion, and over-rode for any who were abroad that night and invoked their aid, the protective Providence of Almight God. Witches, therefore, above all, were peculiarly potent. On this night any witch could entice to herself the heart and the love of any young man who consulted her on matters of philtre or love charm, with the result that on any night in succeeding years of the same date, he, though he was lawfully affianced and wedded, would for that night be hers. If, however, he should call on the name of God through any sudden grace of the Spirit, her charm would be of no avail. On this night, too, all witches had the power by certain dreadful incantations and indescribable profanities, to raise from the dead those who had committed suicide.'

'Top of the next page,' said Hugh. 'Leave out this next paragraph; it does not bear on this last.'

'Near a small village in this country,' I read, 'called Gavon, the moon at midnight is said to shine through a certain gap or fissure in a wall of rock close beside the river on to the ruins of a Pict castle, so that the light of its beams falls on to a large flat stone erected there near the gate and supposed by some to be an ancient and pagan altar. At that moment, so the superstition still lingers in the countryside, the evil and malignant spirits which hold sway on Gavon's Eve, are at the zenith of their powers, and those who invoke their aid at this moment and in this place, will, though with infinite peril to their immortal souls, get all that they desire of them.'

The paragraph on the subject ended here, and I shut the book.

'Well?' I asked.

'Under favourable circumstances two and two make four,' said Hugh.

'And four means –'

'This. Sandy is certainly in consultation with a woman who is supposed to be a witch, whose path no crofter will cross after nightfall. He wants to learn, at whatever cost, poor devil, what happened to Catrine. Thus, I think it more than possible that tomorrow, at midnight, there be folk by the Picts' pool. There is another curious thing. I was fishing there yesterday, and just opposite the river gate of the castle, someone has set up a great flat stone, which has been dragged (for I noticed the crushed grass) from the débris at the bottom of the slope.'

'You mean that the old hag is going to try to raise the body of Catrine, if she is dead?'

'Yes, and I mean to see myself what happens. Come too.'

The next day Hugh and I fished down the river from the lodge, taking with us not Sandy, but another gillie, and ate our lunch on the slope of the Picts' Castle after landing a couple of fish there. Even as Hugh had said, a great flat slab of stone had been dragged on to the platform outside the river gate of the castle, where it rested on certain rude supports, which, now that it was in place, seemed certainly designed to receive it. It was also exactly opposite that lancet window in the basaltic rock across the pool, so that if the moon at midnight did shine through it, the light would fall on the stone. This, then, was the almost certain scene of the incantations.

Below the platform, as I have said, the ground fell rapidly away to the level of the pool, which owing to rain on the hills was running very high, and, streaked with lines of greyish bubbles, poured down in amazing and ear-filling volume. But directly underneath the steep escarpment of rock on the far side of the pool it lay foamless and black, a still backwater of great depth. Above the alter-like erection again the ground rose up seven rough-hewn steps to the gate itself, on each side of which, to the height of about four feet, ran the circular wall of the castle. Inside again were the remains of partition walls between the three chambers, and it was in the one nearest to the river gate that we determined to conceal ourselves that night. From there, should the witch and Sandy keep tryst at the altar, any sound of movement would reach us, and through the aperture of the gate itself we could see, concealed in the shadow of the wall, whatever took place at the altar or down below at the pool. The lodge, finally, was but a short ten minutes away, if one went in the direct line, so that by starting at a quarter to twelve that night, we could enter the Picts' Castle by the gate away from the river, thus not betraying our presence to those who might be waiting for the moment when the moon should shine through the lancet window in the wall of rock on to the altar in front of the river gate.

Night fell very still and windless, and when not long before midnight we let ourselves silently out of the lodge, though to the east the sky was clear, a black continent of cloud was creeping up from the west, and had now nearly reached the zenith. Out of the remote fringes of it, occasional lightning winked, and the growl of very distant thunder sounded drowsily at long intervals after. But it seemed to me as if another storm hung over our heads, ready every moment to burst, for the oppression in the air was of a far heavier quality than so distant a disturbance could have accounted for. To the east, however, the sky was still luminously clear; the curiously hard edges of the western cloud were star-embroidered, and by the dove-coloured light in the east it was evident that the moonrise over the moor was imminent. And though I did not in my heart believe that our expedition would end in anything but yawns, I was conscious of an extreme tension and rawness of nerves, which I set down to the thunder-charged air.

For noiselessness of footstep we had both put on india-rubber soled shoes, and all the way down to the pool we heard nothing but the distant thunder and our own padded tread. Very silently and cautiously we ascended the steps of the gate away from the river, and keeping close to the wall inside,

sidled round to the river gate and peered out. For the first
moment I could see nothing, so black lay the shadow of the
rock-wall opposite across the pool, but by degrees I made out
the lumps and line of the glimmering foam which streaked
the water. High as the river was running this morning it was
infinitely more voluminous and turbulent now, and the sound
of it filled and bewildered the ear with its sonorous roaring.
Only under the very base of the rock opposite it ran quite
black and un-flecked by foam: there lay the deep still surface
of the backwater. Then suddenly I saw something black move
in the dimness in front of me, and against the grey foam rose
up first the head, then the shoulders, and finally the whole figure of a woman coming towards us up the bank. Behind her
walked another, a man and the two came to where the altar of
stone had been newly erected and stood there side by side, sil-
houetted against the churned white of the stream. Hugh had
seen, too, and touched me on the arm to call my attention.
So far then he was right: there was no mistaking the stalwart
proportions of Sandy.

Suddenly across the gloom shot a tiny spear of light, and
momentarily as we watched, it grew larger and longer, till a
tall beam, as from some window cut in the rock opposite, was
shed on the bank below us. It moved slowly, imperceptibly to
the left till it struck full between the two black figures standing there, and shone with a curious bluish gleam on the flat

stone in front of them. Then the roar of the river was suddenly overscored by a dreadful screaming voice, the voice of a woman, and from her side her arms shot up and out as if in invocation of some power. At first I could catch none of the words, but soon from repetition they began to convey an intelligible message to my brain, and I was listening as in the paralytic horror of nightmare to a bellowing of the most hideous and unnameable profanity. What I heard I cannot bring myself to record; suffice it to say that Satan was invoked by every adoring and reverent name, that cursing and unspeakable malediction was poured forth on Him whom we hold most holy. Then the yelling voice ceased as suddenly as it had begun, and for a moment there was silence again, but for the reverberating river.

Then once more that horror of sound was uplifted.

'So, Catrine Gordon,' it cried, 'I bid ye in the name of my master and yours to rise from where ye lie. Up with ye – up!'

Once more there was silence; then I heard Hugh at my elbow draw a quick sobbing breath, and his finger pointed unsteadily to the dead black water below the rock. And I too looked and saw.

Right under the rock there appeared a pale subaqueous light, which waved and quivered in the stream. At first it was very small and dim, but as we looked it seemed to swim upwards from remote depths and grew larger till I suppose the space of some square yard was illuminated by it. Then the surface of the water was broken, and a head, the head of a girl, dead-white and with long, flowing hair, appeared above the stream. Her eyes were shut, the corners of her mouth drooped as in sleep, and the moving water stood in a frill round her neck. Higher and higher rose the figure out of the tide, till at last it stood, luminous in itself, so it appeared, up to the middle. The head was bent down over the breast, and the hands clasped together. As it emerged from the water it seemed to get nearer, and was by now half-way across the pool, moving quietly and steadily against the great flood of the hurrying river.

Then I heard a man's voice crying out in a sort of strangled agony.

'Catrine!' it cried: 'Catrine! In God's name: in God's name!'

In two strides Sandy had rushed down the steep bank, and hurled himself out into that mad swirl of waters. For one moment I saw his arms flung up into the sky, the next he had altogether gone. And on the utterance of the Name that unholy vision had vanished too, while simulatneously there burst in front of us a light so blinding, followed by a crack of thunder so appalling to the senses, that I know I just hid my face in my hands. At once, as if the flood-gates of the sky had been opened the deluge was on us, not like rain, but like one sheet of solid water, so that we cowered under it. Any hope or attempt to rescue Sandy was out of the question; to dive into that whirlpool of mad water meant instant death, and even had it been possible for any swimmer to live there in the blackness of the night there was absolutely no chance of finding him. Besides, even if it had been possible to save him, I doubt whether I was sufficiently master of my flesh and blood as to endure to plunge where that apparition had risen.

Then, as we lay there, another horror filled and possessed my mind. Somewhere close to us in the darkness was that woman whose yelling voice just now had made my blood run ice-cold, while it brought the streaming sweat to my forehead. At that moment I turned to Hugh.

'I cannot stop here,' I said. 'I must run, run right away. Where is She?'

'Did you not see?' he asked.

'No. What happened?'

'The lightning struck the stone within a few inches of where she was standing. We – we must go and look for her.'

I followed him down the slope, shaking as if I had the palsy, and groping with my hands on the ground in front of me, in deadly terror of encountering something human. The thunderclouds had in the last few minutes spread over the moon, so that no ray from the window in the rock guided our search. But up and down the bank from the stone that lay shattered there to the edge of the pool we groped and stumbled, but found nothing. At length we gave it up: it seemed morally certain that she, too, had rolled down the bank after the lighting stroke, and lay somewhere deep in the pool from which she had called the dead.

None fished the pool next day, but men with dragnets came from Brora. Right under the rock in the backwater lay two bodies, close together, Sandy and the dead girl. Of the other they found nothing.

It would seem, then, that Catrine Gordon, in answer to Sandy's letter, left Inverness in heavy trouble. What happened afterwards can only be conjectured, but it seems likely she took the short cut to Gavon, meaning to cross the river on the boulders above the Picts' pool. But whether she slipped accidentally in her passage, and so was drawn down by the hungry water, or whether, unable to face the future, she had thrown herself into the pool, we can only guess. In any case they sleep together now in the bleak, wind-swept graveyard at Brora, in obedience to the inscrutable designs of God.

THE SANCTUARY

Francis Elton was spending a fortnight's holiday one January in the Engadine, when he received the telegram announcing the death of his uncle, Horace Elton, and his own succession to a very agreeable property: the telegram added that the cremation of the remains was to take place that day, and it was therefore impossible for him to attend, and there was no reason for his hurrying home.

In the solicitor's letter that reached him two days later Mr. Angus gave fuller details: the estate consisted of sound securities to the value of about £80,000, and there was as well Mr. Elton's property just outside the small country town of Wedder-burn in Hampshire. This consisted of a charming house and garden and a small acreage of building land. Everything had been left to Francis, but the estate was saddled with a charge of £500 a year in favour of the Reverend Owen Barton.

Francis knew very little of his uncle, who for a long time had been much of a recluse; indeed he had not seen him for nearly four years, when he had spent three days with him at this house at Wedderburn. He had vague but slightly uneasy memories of those days, and now on his journey home, as he lay in his berth in the rocking train, his brain, rummaging drowsily among its buried recollections, began to disinter these. There was nothing very definite about them: they consisted of suggestions and side-lights and oblique impressions, things observed, so to speak, out of the corner of his eye, and never examined in direct focus.

He had only been a boy at the time, having just left school, and it was in the summer holidays, hot sultry weather of August, he remembered, that he had paid him this visit, before he went to a crammer's in London to learn French and German.

There was his Uncle Horace, first of all, and of him he had vivid images. A grey-haired man of middle age, large and extremely stout with a cushion of jowl overlapping his collar, but in spite of this obesity, he was nimble and light in movement, and with a merry blue eye that was equally alert, and seemed constantly to be watching him. Then there were two women there, a mother and daughter, and, as he recalled them, their names occurred to him, too: they were Mrs. Isabel Ray and Judith. Judith, he supposed, was a year or two older than himself, and on the first evening had taken him for a stroll in the garden after dinner. She had treated him at once as if they were old friends, had walked with her arm round his neck, had asked him many questions about his school, and whether there was any girl he was keen on. All very friendly, but rather embarrassing. When they came in from the garden, certainly some questioning signal had passed between the mother and the girl, and Judith had shrugged her shoulders in reply.

Then the mother had taken him in hand; she made him sit with her in the window-seat, and talked to him about the crammer's he was going to: he would have much more liberty, she supposed, than he had at school, and he looked the sort of boy who would make good use of it. She tried him in French and found he could speak it very decently, and told him that she had a book which she had just finished, which she would lend him. It was by that exquisite stylist Huysman and was called *Là-Bas*. She would not tell him what it was about: he must find out for himself. All the time those narrow grey eyes were fixed on him, and when she went to bed, she took him up to her room to give him the book. Judith was there, too: she had read it, and laughed at the memory of it. 'Read it, darling Francis,' she said, 'and then go to sleep immediately, and you will tell me tomorrow what you dreamed about, unless it would shock me.'

The vibrating rhythm of the train made Francis drowsy, but his mind went on disinterring these fragments. There had been another man there, his uncle's secretary, a young fellow, perhaps twenty-five years old, clean-shaven and slim and with just the same gaiety about him as the rest. Everyone treated him with an odd sort of deference, hard to define but easy to perceive. He sat next to Francis at dinner that night, and kept filling his wine-glass for him whether he wanted it or not, and next morning he had come into his room in pyjamas, sat on his bed, looked at him with odd questioning eyes, had asked him how he got on with his book, and then taken him to bathe in the swimming-pool behind the belt of trees at the bottom of the garden. . . . No bathing-costume, he said, was necessary, and they raced up and down the pool and lay basking in the sun afterwards. Then from the belt of trees emerged Judith and her mother, and Francis, much embarrassed, draped himself in a towel. How they all laughed at his delightful prudery. . . . And what was the man's name? Why, of course, it was Owen Barton, the same who had been mentioned in Mr. Angus's letter as the Reverend Owen Barton. But why 'reverend', Francis wondered. Perhaps he had taken Orders afterwards.

All day they had flattered him for his good looks, and his swimming and his lawn-tennis: he had never been made so much of, and all their eyes were on him, inviting and beckoning. In the afternoon his uncle had claimed him: he must come upstairs with him and see some of his treasures. He took him into his bedroom, and opened a great wardrobe full of magnificent vestments. There were gold-embroidered copes, there were stoles and chasubles with panels of needlework enriched with pearls, and jewelled gloves, and the use of them was to make glorious the priests who offered prayer and praise to the Lord of all things visible and invisible. Then he brought out a scarlet cassock of thick shimmering silk, and a cotta of finest muslin trimmed round the neck and the lower hem with Irish lace of the sixteenth century. These were for the vesting of the boy who served at the Mass, and Francis, at his uncle's bidding, stripped off his coat and arrayed himself, and took off his shoes and put on the noiseless scarlet slippers which were called sanctuary shoes. Then Owen Barton entered, and Francis heard him whisper to his uncle, 'God! What a server!' and then he put on one of those gorgeous copes and told him to kneel.

The boy had been utterly bewildered. What were they playing at, he wondered. Was it charades of some sort? There was Barton, his face solemn and eager, raising his left hand as if in blessing: more astonishing was his uncle, licking his lips and swallowing in his throat, as if his mouth watered. There was something below all this dressing-up, which meant nothing to him, but had some hidden significance for the two men. It was uncomfortable: it disquieted him, and he wouldn't kneel, but disrobed himself of the cotta and cassock. 'I don't know what it's about,' he said: and again, as between Judith and her mother, he saw question and answer pass between them. Somehow his lack of interest had disappointed them, but he felt no interest at all: just a vague repulsion.

The diversions of the day were renewed: there was more tennis and bathing, but they all seemed to have lost the edge of their keenness about him. That evening he was dressed rather earlier than the others, and was sitting in a deep window-seat of the drawing-room, reading the book Mrs. Ray had lent him. He was not getting on with it; it was puzzling, and the French was difficult: he thought he would return it to her, saying that it was beyond him. Just then she and his uncle entered: they were talking together, and did not perceive him.

'No, it's no use, Isabel,' said his uncle. 'He's got no curiosity, no leanings: it would only disgust him and put him off. That's not the way to win souls. Owen thinks so, too. And he's too innocent: why when I was his age . . . Why, there's Francis. What's the boy reading? Ah, I see! What do you make of it?'

Francis closed the book.

'I give it up,' he said. 'I can't get on with it.'

Mrs. Ray laughed.

'I agree, too, Horace,' she said. 'But what a pity!'

Somehow Francis got the impression, he remembered, that they had been talking about him. But, if so, *what* was it for which he had no leanings?'

He had gone to bed rather early that night, encouraged, he thought, to do so, leaving the rest at a game of Bridge. He soon slept, but awoke, thinking he heard the sound of chanting. Then came three strokes of a bell, and a pause and three more. He was too sleepy to care what it was about.

Such, as the train rushed through the night, was the sum of his impressions about his visit to the man whose substance he had now inherited, subject to the charge of £500 a year to the Reverend Owen Barton. He was astonished to find how vivid and how vaguely disquieting were these memories, which now for four years had been buried in his mind. As he sank into sounder sleep they faded again, and he thought little more of them in the morning.

He went to see Mr. Angus as soon as he got to London. Certain securities would have to be sold in order to pay death duties, but the administration of the estate was a simple matter. Francis wanted to know more about his benefactor, but Mr. Angus could tell him very little. Horace Elton had, for some years, lived an extremely sequestered life down at Wedderburn, and his only intimate associate was his secretary, this Mr. Owen Barton. Beyond him, there were two ladies who used often to stay with him for long periods. Their names?—and he paused, searching his memory.

'Mrs. Isabel Ray and her daughter Judith?' suggested Francis.

'Exactly. They were often there. And, not infrequently, a number of people used to arrive rather late in the evening, eleven o'clock or even later, stay for an hour or two and then be off again. A little mysterious. Only a week or so before Mr. Elton died, there had been quite a congregation of them, fifteen or twenty, I believe.'

Francis was silent for a moment: it was as if pieces of jigsaw puzzle were calling for their due location. But their shapes were too fantastic. . . .

'And about my uncle's illness and death,' he said. 'The cremation of his body was on the same day as that on which he died; at least so I understood from your telegram.'

'Yes: that was so,' said Mr. Angus.

'But why? I should instantly have come back to England in order to be present. Was it not unusual?'

'Yes, Mr. Elton, it was unusual. But there were reasons for it.'

'I should like to hear them,' he said. 'I was his heir, and it would have been only proper that I should have been there. Why?'

Angus hesitated a moment.

'That is a reasonable question,' he said, 'and I feel bound to answer it. I must begin a little way back. . . . Your Uncle was in excellent physical health apparently, till about a week before his death. Very stout, but very alert and active. Then the trouble began. It took the form at first of some grievous mental and spiritual disturbance. He thought for some reason that he was going to die very soon, and the idea of death produced in him an abnormal panic terror. He telegraphed for me, for he wanted to make some alteration in his will. I was away and could not get down till the next day, and by the time I arrived he was too desperately ill to give any sort of coherent instructions. But his intention, I think, was to cut Mr. Owen Barton out of it.'

Again the lawyer paused.

'I found,' he said, 'that on the morning of the day I got down to Wedderburn, he had sent for the parson of his parish, and had made a confession to him. What that was I have not, of course, the slightest idea. Till then he had been in this panic fear of death, but was physically himself. Immediately afterwards some very horrible disease invaded him. Just that: invasion. The doctors who were summoned from London and Bournemouth had no idea what it was. Some unknown microbe, they supposed, which made the most swift and frightful havoc of skin and tissue and bone. It was like some putrefying internal corruption. It was as if he was dead already. . . . Really, I don't know what good it will do to tell you this.'

'I want to know,' said Francis.

'Well: this corruption. Living organisms came out as from a dead body. His nurses used to be sick. And the room was always swarming with flies; great fat flies, crawling over the walls and the bed. He was quite conscious, and there persisted this frantic terror of death, when you would have thought that a man's soul would have been only too thankful to be quit of such a habitation.'

'And was Mr. Owen Barton with him?' asked Francis.

'From the moment that Mr. Elton made his confession, he refused to see him. Once he came into the room, and there was a shocking scene. The dying man screamed and yelled with terror. Nor would he see the two ladies we have mentioned: why they continued to stop in the house I can't imagine. Then on the last morning of his life—he could not speak now—he traced a word or two on a piece of paper, and it seemted that he wanted to receive the Holy Communion. So the parson was sent for.'

The old lawyer paused again: Francis saw that his hand was shaking:

'Then very dreadful things happened,' he said. 'I was in the room, for he signed to me to be near him, and I saw them with my own eyes. The parson had poured the wine into the chalice, and had put the bread on the paten, and was about to consecrate the elements, when a cloud of those flies, of which I have told you, came about him. They filled the chalice like a swarm of bees, they settled in their unclean thousands on the paten, and in a couple of minutes the chalice was dry and empty and they had devoured the bread. Then like drilled hosts, you may say, they swarmed on to your uncle's face, so that you could see nothing of it. He choked and he gasped:

there was one writhing convulsion, and, thank God, it was all over.'

'And then?' asked Francis.

'There were no flies. Nothing. But it was necessary to have the body cremated at once and the bedding with it. Very shocking indeed! I would not have told you, if you had not pressed me.'

'And the ashes?' asked he.

'You will see that there is a clause in his will, directing that his remains should be buried at the foot of the Judas-tree beside the swimming pool in the garden at Wedderburn. That was done.'

Francis was a very unimaginative young man, free from superstitious twitterings and unprofitable speculations, and this story, suggestive though it was, of ghastly sub-currents, did not take hold of his mind at all or lead to the fashioning of uneasy fancies. It was all very horrible, but it was over. He went down to Wedderburn for Easter with a widowed sister of his and her small boy, aged eleven, and they all fairly fell in love with the place. It was soon settled that Sybil Marsham should let her house in London for the summer months, and establish herself here. Dickie, who was a delicate boy, rather queer and elfin, would thus have the benefit of country air, and Francis the benefit of having the place run by his sister and occupied and in commission whenever he was able to get away from his work.

The house was of brick and timber, with accommodation for half a dozen folk, and stood on high ground above the little town. Francis made a tour of it, as soon as he arrived, rather astonished to find how the sight of it rubbed up to clearness in the minutest details his memory of it. There was the sitting-room with its tall bookcases and its deep window-seats over-looking the garden, where he had sat unobserved when his uncle and Mrs. Ray came in talking together. Above was his uncle's panelled bedroom, which he proposed to occupy himself, with the big wardrobe containing vestments. He opened it: they were under their covering sheets of tissue paper, shimmering with scarlet and gold and finest lawn foamed with Irish lace: a faint smell of incense hung about them. Next there was his uncle's sitting-room, and beyond that the room which he had slept in before, and was now appropriated to Dickie. These rooms lay on the front of the house, looking westwards over the garden, and he went out to renew acquaintance with it. Flower-beds gay with spring blossoms ran below the windows: then came the lawn, and beyond the belt of trees that enclosed the swimming pool. He passed along the path that threaded it between tapestries of primrose and anemone, and came out into the clearing that surrounded the water. The bathing shed stood at the deep end of it by the sluice that splashed riotously into the channel below, for the stream that supplied the pool was running full with the rains of March. In front of the copse on the far side stood a Judas-tree decked gloriously with flowers, and the reflection of it was cast waveringly on the rippled surface of the water. Somewhere below those red-blossoming boughs, there was buried a casket of ashes. He strolled round the pool: it was quite sheltered here from the April breeze, and bees were busy in the red blossoms. Bees, and large fat flies, a quantity of them.

He and Sybil were sitting in the drawing-room with the deep window-seats as dusk began to fall. A servant came in to say that Mr. Owen Barton had called. Certainly they were at home, and he entered, and was introduced to Sybil.

'You will hardly remember me, Mr. Elton,' he said, 'but I was here when you paid a visit to your uncle: four years ago it must have been.'

'But I remember you perfectly,' he said. 'We bathed together, we played tennis: you were very kind to a shy boy. And are you living here still?'

'Yes: I took a house in Wedderburn after your uncle's death. I spent six very happy years with him as his secretary, and I got much attached to the country. My house stands just outside your garden palings opposite the latched gate leading into the wood round the pool.'

The door opened and Dickie came in. He caught sight of

the stranger and stopped.

'Say "how do you do" to Mr. Barton, Dickie,' said his mother.

Dickie performed this duty with due politeness and stood regarding him. He was a shy boy usually; but, after this inspection, he advanced close to him, and laid his hands on his knees.

'I like you,' he said confidently, and leant up against him.

'Don't bother Mr. Barton, Dickie,' she said rather sharply.

'But indeed he's doing nothing of the kind,' said Barton, and he drew the boy towards him so that he stood clipped between his knees.

Sybil got up.

'Come, Dick,' she said. 'We'll have a walk round the garden before it gets dark.'

'Is he coming, too?' asked the boy.

'No: he's going to stop and talk to Uncle Francis.'

When the two men were alone Barton said a word or two about Horace Elton, who had always been so generous a friend to him. The end, mercifully short, had been terrible, and terrible to him personally had been the dying man's refusal to see him during the last two days of his life.

'His mind, I think, must have been affected,' he said, 'by his awful sufferings. It happens like that sometimes: people

turn against those with whom they have been most intimate. I have often mourned over that, and deeply regretted
it. . . . And I owe you a certain word of explanation, Mr.
Elton. No doubt you were puzzled to find in your uncle's will
that I was entitled "the Reverend". It is quite true, though I
do not call myself so. Certain spiritual doubts and difficulties
caused me to give up my orders, but your uncle always held
that if a man is once a priest he is always a priest. He was very
strong about that, and no doubt he was right.'

'I didn't know my uncle took any interest in ecclesiastical
affairs,' said Francis. 'Ah, I had forgotten about his vestments.
Perhaps that was only an artistic taste.'

'By no means. He regarded them as sacred things, consecrated to holy uses. . . . And may I ask you what happened
to his remains? I remember he once expressed a wish to be
buried by the swimming pool.'

'His body was cremated,' said Francis, 'and the ashes were
buried there.'

Barton stayed but little longer, and Sybil on her return was
frankly relieved to find he had gone. Simply, she didn't like
him. There was something queer, something sinister about
him. Francis laughed at her: quite a good fellow, he thought.

Dreams, of course, are a mere hash-up of recent mental
images and associations, and a very vivid dream that came to
Francis that night could easily have arisen from such topics.

He thought he was swimming in the bathing pool with Owen Barton, and that his uncle, stout and florid, was standing underneath the Judas-tree watching them. That seemed quite natural, as is the way of dreams: merely he was not dead at all. When they came out of the water, he looked for his clothes, but found that there was laid out for him a scarlet cassock and a white lace-trimmed cotta. This again was quite natural; so, too, was the fact that Barton put on a gold cope.

His uncle, very merry and licking his lips, joined them, and each of them took an arm of his and they walked back to the house together singing a hymn. As they went the daylight died, and by the time they crossed the lawn it was black night, and the windows of the house were lit. They walked upstairs, still singing, into his uncle's bedroom which was now his own. There was an open door, which he had never noticed before opposite his bed, and there came a very bright light from it. Then the sense of nightmare began, for his two companions, gripping him tightly, pulled him along towards it, and he struggled with them knowing there was something terrible within. But step by step they dragged him, violently resisting, and now out of the door there came a swarm of large fat flies that buzzed and settled on him. Thicker and thicker they streamed out, covering his face, and crawling into his eyes, and entering his mouth as he panted for breath. The horror grew to breaking-point, and he woke sweating with a hammering heart. He switched on the light, and there was the quiet room and the dawn beginning to be luminous outside, and the birds just tuning up.

Francis's few days of holiday passed quickly. He went down to the village to see Barton's house, and found it a most pleasant little dwelling, and its owner an exceedingly pleasant fellow. Barton dined with them one evening, and Sybil went so far as to admit that her first judgment of him was hasty. He was charming with Dickie, too, and that disposed her in his favour, and the boy adored him. Soon it was necessary to find some tutor for him, and Barton readily agreed to undertake his education, and every morning Dickie trotted across the garden and through the wood where the swimming pool lay to Barton's house. His ill-health had made him rather backward in his studies, but he was now eager to learn and to please his instructor, and he got on quickly.

✳   ✳   ✳

It was now that I first met Francis, and during the next few months in London we became close friends. He told me that he had lately inherited this place at Wedderburn from his uncle, but for the present I knew no more than that of the previous history which I have just recorded. Sometime during July he told me he was intending to spend the month of August there. His sister, who kept house for him, and her small boy would be away for the first week or two, for she had taken

him off to the seaside. Would I then come and share his soli-
tude, and get on there, uninterrupted, with some work I had
on hand. That seemed a very attractive plan, and we motored
down together one very hot afternoon early in August, that
promised thunder. Owen Barton, he told me, who had been
his uncle's secretary, was coming to dine with us that night.

It wanted an hour or so yet to dinner-time when we arrived, and Francis directed me, if I cared for a dip, to the bathing pool among the trees beyond the lawn. He had various
household businesses to look into himself, so I went off alone.
It was an enchanting place, the water still and very clear, mir-
roring the sky and the full-foliaged trees, and I stripped and
plunged in. I lay and floated in the cool water, I swam and
dived again, and then I saw, walking close to the far bank
of the pool, a man of something more than middle-age, and
extremely stout. He was in dress clothes, dinner-jacket and
black tie, and instantly it struck me that this must be Mr.
Barton coming up from the village to dine with us. It must
therefore be later than I thought, and I swam back to the
shed where my clothes were. As I climbed out of the water, I
glanced round. There was no one there.

It was a slight shock, but very slight. It was odd that he
should have come so unexpectedly out of the wood and disappeared again so suddenly, but it did not concern me much.
I hurried home, changed quickly and came down, expecting

to find Francis and his guest in the drawing-room. But I need not have been in such haste for now my watch told me that there was still a quarter of an hour before dinner-time. As for the others, I supposed that Mr. Barton was upstairs with Francis in his sitting-room. So I picked up a chance book to beguile the time, and read for a while, but the room grew rather dark, and, rising to switch on the electric light, I saw standing outside the french window into the garden the figure of a man, outlined against the last of a stormy sunset, looking into the room.

There was no doubt whatever in my mind that he was the same person as I had seen when I was bathing, and the switching on of the light made this clear, for it shone full on his face. No doubt then Mr. Barton finding he was too early was strolling about the garden till the dinner-hour. But now I did not look forward at all to this evening: I had had a good look at him and there was something horrible about him. Was he human, was he earthly at all? Then he quietly moved away, and immediately afterwards there came a knock at the front door just outside the room, and I heard Francis coming downstairs. He went to the door himself: there was a word of greeting, and he came into the room accompanied by a tall, slim fellow whom he introduced to me.

We had a very pleasant evening: Barton talked fluently and agreeably, and more than once he spoke of his friend and pu-

pil Dickie. About eleven he rose to go, and Francis suggested
to him that he should walk back across the garden which gave
him a short cut to his house. The threatening storm still held
off, but it was very dark overhead, as we stood together outside the french window. Barton was soon swallowed up in the
blackness. Then there came a bright flash of lightning, and in
that moment of illumination I saw that there was standing in
the middle of the lawn, as if waiting for him, the figure I had
seen twice already. 'Who is that?' was on the tip of my tongue,
but instantly I perceived that Francis had seen nothing of it,
and so I was silent, for I knew now what I had already half-
guessed that this was no living man of flesh and blood whom
I had seen. A few heavy drops of rain plopped on the flagged
walk, and, as we moved indoors, Francis called out, 'Good
night, Barton!' and the cheery voice answered.

Before long we went up to bed, and he took me into his
room as we passed, a big panelled chamber with a great wardrobe by the bed. Close to it hung an oil-portrait of kit-cat
size.

'I'll show you what's in that wardrobe tomorrow,' he said.
'Rather wonderful things. . . . That's a picture of my uncle.'

I had seen that face before this evening.

For the next two or three days I had no further glimpse of
that dreadful visitant, but never for a moment was I at ease,
for I was aware that he was about. What instinct or what sense

perceived that, I have no idea: perhaps it was merely the dread I had of seeing him again that gave rise to the conviction. I thought of telling Francis that I must get back to London; what prevented me from so doing was the desire to know more, and that made me fight this cold fear. Then very soon I perceived that Francis was no more at ease than I was. Sometimes as we sat together in the evening he was oddly alert: he would pause in the middle of a sentence as if some sound had attracted his attention, or he would look up from our game of bezique and focus his eyes for a second on some corner of the room or, more often, on the dark oblong of the open french window. Had he, I wondered, been seeing something invisible to me, and, like myself, feared to speak of it?

These impressions were momentary and infrequent, but they kept alive in me the feeling that there was something astir, and that something, coming out of the dark and the unknown, was growing in force. It had come into the house, and was present everywhere. . . . And then one awoke again to a morning of heavenly brightness and sunshine, and surely one was disquieting oneself in vain.

I had been there about a week when something occurred which precipitated what followed. I slept in the room which Dickie usually occupied, and awoke one night feeling uncomfortably hot. I tugged at a blanket to remove it, but it was tucked very tightly in between the mattresses on the side of the bed next to the wall. Eventually I got it free, and as I did so I heard something drop with a flutter on to the floor. In the morning I remembered that, and found underneath the bed a little paper notebook. I opened it idly enough, and within were a dozen pages written over in a round childish handwriting, and these words struck my eye:

'Thursday, July 11th. I saw great-uncle Horace again this morning in the wood. He told me something about myself which I didn't understand, but he said I should like it when I got older. I mustn't tell anybody that he's here, nor what he told me, except Mr. Barton.'

I did not care one jot whether I was reading a boy's private diary. That was no longer a consideration worth thinking about. I turned over the page and found another entry.

'Sunday, July 21st. I saw Uncle Horace again. I said I had told Mr. Barton what he had told me, and Mr. Barton had told me some more things, and that he was pleased, and said I was getting on and that he would take me to prayers some day soon.'

I cannot describe the thrill of horror that these entries woke in me. They made the apparition which I had seen infinitely more real and more sinister. It was a spirit corrupt and malign and intent on corruption that haunted the place. But what was I to do? How could I, without any lead from Francis, tell him that the spirit of his uncle—of whom at present

I knew nothing—had been seen not by me only, but by his nephew, and that he was at work on the boy's mind? Then there was the mention of Barton. Certainly that could not be left as it was. He was collaborating in that damnable task. A cult of corruption (or was I being too fantastic?) began to outline itself. Then what did that sentence about taking him to prayers mean? But Dickie was away, thank goodness, for the present, and there was time to think it over. As for that pitiful little notebook, I put it into a locked despatch case.

The day, as far as outward and visible signs were concerned, passed pleasantly. For me there was a morning's work, and for both of us an afternoon on the golf-links. But below there was something heavy; my knowledge of that diary kept intervening with mental telephone-calls asking 'What are you going to *do*?' Francis, on his side, was troubled; there were sub-currents, and I did not know what they were. Silences fell, not the natural unobserved silences between those who are intimate, which are only a symbol of their intimacy, but the silences between those who have something on their minds of which they fear to speak. These had got more stringent all day: there was a growing tenseness: all common topics were banal, for they only cloaked a certain topic.

We sat out on the lawn before dinner on that sultry evening, and breaking one of these silent intervals, he pointed at the front of the house.

'There's an odd thing,' he said. 'Look! There are three rooms aren't there on the ground floor: dining-room, drawing-room, and the little study where you write. Now look above. There are three rooms there: your bedroom, my bedroom, and my sitting-room. I've measured them. There are twelve feet missing. Looks as if there was a sealed-up room somewhere.'

Here, at any rate, was something to talk about.

'Exciting,' I said. 'Mayn't we explore?'

'We will. We'll explore as soon as we've dined. Then there's another thing: quite off the point. You remember those vestments I showed you the other day? I opened the wardrobe, where they are kept, an hour ago, and a lot of big fat flies came buzzing out. A row like a dozen aeroplanes overhead. Remote but loud, if you know what I mean. And then there weren't any.'

Somehow I felt that what we had been silent about was coming out into the open. It might be ill to look upon. . . .

He jumped from his chair.

'Let's have done with these silences,' he cried. 'He's here, my uncle, I mean. I haven't told you yet, but he died in a swarm of flies. He asked for the Sacrament, but before the wine was consecrated the chalice was choked with them. And I know he's here. It sounds damned rot, but he is.'

'I know that, too,' I said. 'I've seen him.'

'Why didn't you tell me?'

126

'Because I thought you would laugh at me.'

'I should have a few days ago,' said he. 'But I don't now. Go on.'

'The first evening I was here I saw him at the bathing pool. That same night, when we were seeing Owen Barton off, a flash of lightning came, and he was there again standing on the lawn.'

'But how did you know it was he?' asked Francis.

'I knew it when you showed me the portrait of him in your bedroom that same night. Have you seen him?'

'No; but he's here. Anything more?'

This was the opportunity not only natural but inevitable.

'Yes, much more,' I said. 'Dickie has seen him too.'

'That child? Impossible.'

The door out of the drawing-room opened, and Francis's parlour-maid came out with the sherry on a tray. She put the decanter and glasses down on the wicker table between us, and I asked her to bring out the despatch case from my room. I took the paper notebook out of it.

'This slipped out from between my mattresses last night. It's Dickie's diary. Listen': and I read him the first extract.

Francis gave one of those swift disconcerting glances over his shoulder.

'But we're dreaming,' he said. 'It's a nightmare. God, there's something awful here! And what about Dickie not telling anybody except Barton what he told him? Anything more?'

'Yes. "Sunday, July 21st. I saw Uncle Horace again. I said I had told Mr. Barton what he told me, and Mr. Barton told me some more things, and that he was pleased and said I was getting on, and that he would take me to prayers some day soon. I don't know what that means." '

Francis sprang out of his chair.

'What?' he cried. 'Take him to prayers? Wait a minute. Let me remember about my first visit here. I was a boy of nineteen, and frightfully, absurdly innocent for my age. A woman staying here gave me a book to read called *Là-Bas*. I didn't get far in it then, but I know what it's about now.'

'Black Mass,' said I. 'Satan worshippers.'

'Yes. Then one day my uncle dressed me up in a scarlet cassock, and Barton came in and put on a cope and said something about my being a server. He used to be a priest, did you know that? And one night I awoke and heard the sound of chanting and a bell rang. By the way, Barton's coming to dine tomorrow. . . .'

'What are you going to do?'

'About him? I can't tell yet. But we've got something to do tonight. Horrors have happened here in this house. There must be some room where they held their Mass, a chapel. Why, there's that missing space I spoke of just now.'

After dinner we set to work. Somewhere on the first floor

on the garden front of the house there was this space unaccounted for by the dimensions of the rooms there. We turned on the electric light in all of them, and then going out into the garden we saw that the windows in Francis's bedroom and in his sitting-room next door were far more widely spaced than they should have been. Somewhere, then, between them lay the area to which there was no apparent access and we went upstairs. The wall of his sitting-room seemed solid, it was of brick and timber, and large beams ran through it at narrow intervals. But the wall of his bedroom was panelled, and when we tapped on it, no sound came through into the other room beyond.

We began to examine it.

The servants had gone to bed, and the house was silent, but as we moved about from garden to house and from one room to another there was some presence watching and following us. We had shut the door into his bedroom from the passage, but now as we peered and felt about the panelling, the door swung open and closed again, and something entered, brushing my shoulder as it passed.

'What's that?' I said. 'Someone came in.'

'Never mind that,' he said. 'Look what I've found.'

In the border of one of the panels was a black stud like an ebony bell-push. He pressed it and pulled, and a section of the panelling slid sideways, disclosing a red curtain cloaking a doorway. He drew it aside with a clash of metal rings. It was dark within, and out of the darkness came a smell of stale incense. I felt with my hand along the frame of the doorway and found a switch, and the blackness was flooded with a dazzling light.

Within was a chapel. There was no window, and at the West end of it (not the East) there stood an altar. Above it was a picture, evidently of some early Italian school. It was on the lines of the Fra Angelico picture of the Annunciation. The Virgin sat in an open loggia, and on the flowery space outside the angel made his salutation. His spreading wings were the wings of a bat, and his black head and neck were those of a raven. He had his left hand, not his right, raised in blessing. The virgin's robe of thinnest red muslin was trimmed with revolting symbols, and her face was that of a panting dog with tongue protruding.

There were two niches at the East end, in which were marble statues of naked men, with the inscriptions 'St. Judas' and 'St. Gilles de Raies'. One was picking up pieces of silver that lay at his feet, the other looked down leering and laughing at the prone figure of a mutilated boy. The place was lit by a chandelier from the ceiling: this was of the shape of a crown of thorns and electric bulbs nestled among the woven silver twigs. A bell hung from the roof, close beside the altar.

For the moment, as I looked on these obscene blasphemies, I felt that they were merely grotesque and no more to be regarded seriously than the dirty inscriptions written upon empty wall-spaces in the street. That indifference swiftly passed, and a horrified consciousness of the devotion of those who had fashioned and assembled these decorations took its place. Skilled painters and artificers had wrought them and they were here for the service of all that is evil; that spirit of adoration lived in them dynamic and active. And the place was throbbing with the exultant joy of those who had worshipped here.

'And look here!' called Francis. He pointed to a little table standing against the wall just outside the altar-rails.

There were photographs on it, one of a boy standing on the header-board at the bathing pool about to plunge.

'That's me,' he said. 'Barton took it. And what's written underneath it? "Ora pro Francisco Elton." And that's Mrs. Ray, and that's my uncle, and that's Barton in a cope. Pray for him, too, please. But it's childish!'

He suddenly burst into a shout of laughter. The roof of the chapel was vaulted and the echo that came from it was loud and surprising, the place rang with it. His laughter ceased, but not so the echo. There was someone else laughing. But where? Who? Except for us the chapel was empty of all visible presences.

On and on the laughter went, and we stared at each other

with panic stirring. The brilliant light from the chandelier began to fade, dusk gathered, and in the dusk there was brewing some hellish and deadly force. And through the dimness I saw, hanging in the air, and oscillating slightly as if in a draught the laughing face of Horace Elton. Francis saw it too.

'Fight it! Withstand it!' he cried as he pointed to it. 'Desecrate all that it holds sanctified! God, do you smell the incense and the corruption?'

We tore the photographs, we smashed the table on which they stood. We plucked the frontal from the altar and spat on the accursed table: we tugged at it till it toppled over and the marble slab split in half. We hauled from the niches the two statues that stood there, and crash they went on to the paved floor. Then appalled at the riot of our iconoclasm we paused. The laughter had ceased and no oscillating face dangled in the dimness. Then we left the chapel and pulled across the doorway the panel that closed it.

Francis came to sleep in my room, and we talked long, laying our plans for next day. We had forgotten the picture over the altar in our destruction, but now it worked in with what we proposed to do. Then we slept, and the night passed without disturbance. At the least we had broken up the apparatus that was hallowed to unhallowed uses, and that was something. But there was grim work ahead yet, and the issue was unconjecturable.

Barton came to dine that next evening, and there hung on the wall opposite his place the picture from the chapel upstairs. He did not notice it at first, for the room was rather dark, but not dark enough yet to need artificial light. He was gay and lively as usual, spoke amusingly and wittily, and asked when his friend Dickie was to return. Towards the end of dinner the lights were switched on, and then he saw the picture. I was watching him, and the sweat started out on his face that had grown clay-coloured in a moment. Then he pulled himself together.

'That's a strange picture,' he said. 'Was it here before? Surely not.'

'No: it was in a room upstairs,' said Francis. 'About Dickie? I don't know for certain when he'll come back. We have found his diary, and presently we must speak about that.'

'Dickie's diary? Indeed!' said Barton, and he moistened his lips with his tongue.

I think he guessed then that there was something desperate ahead, and I pictured a man condemned to be hanged waiting in his cell with his warders for the imminent hour, as Barton waited then. He sat with an elbow on the table and his hand propping his forehead. Immediately almost the servant brought in our coffee and left us.

'Dickie's diary,' said Francis quietly. 'Your name figures in it. Also my uncle's. Dickie saw him more than once. But, of course, you know that.'

Barton drank off his glass of brandy.

'Are you telling me a ghost story?' he said. 'Pray go on.'

'Yes, it's partly a ghost story, but not entirely. My uncle—his ghost if you like—told him certain stories and said he must keep them secret except from you. And you told him more. And you said he should come to prayers with you some day soon. Where was that to be? In the room just above us?'

The brandy had given the condemned man a momentary courage.

'A pack of lies, Mr. Elton,' he said. 'That boy has got a corrupt mind. He told me things that no boy of his age should know: he giggled and laughed at them. Perhaps I ought to have told his mother.'

'It's too late to think of that now,' said Francis. 'The diary I spoke of will be in the hands of the police at ten o'clock tomorrow morning. They will also inspect the room upstairs where you have been in the habit of celebrating the Black Mass.'

Barton leant forward towards him.

'No, no,' he cried. 'Don't do that! I beg and implore you! I will confess the truth to you. I will conceal nothing. My life has been a blasphemy. But I'm sorry: I repent. I abjure all those abominations from henceforth: I renounce them all in the name of Almighty God.'

'Too late,' said Francis.

And then the horror that haunts me still began to manifest itself. The wretched man threw himself back in his chair, and there dropped from his forehead on to his white shirt-front a long grey worm that lay and wriggled there. At that moment there came from overhead the sound of a bell, and he sprang to his feet.

'No!' he cried again. 'I retract all I said. I abjure nothing. And my Lord is waiting for me in the sanctuary. I must be quick and make my humble confession to him.'

With the movement of a slinking animal he slid from the room, and we heard his steps going swiftly upstairs.

'Did you see?' I whispered. 'And what's to be done? Is the man sane?'

'It's beyond us now,' said Francis.

There was a thump on the ceiling overhead as if someone had fallen, and without a word we ran upstairs into Francis's bedroom. The door of the wardrobe where the vestments were kept was open, some lay on the floor. The panel was open, too, but within it was dark. In terror at what might meet our eyes, I felt for the switch and turned the light on.

The bell which had sounded a few minutes ago was still swinging gently, though speaking no more. Barton, clad in the gold-embroidered cope, lay in front of the overturned altar, with his face twitching. Then that ceased, the rattle of death creaked in his throat, and his mouth fell open. Great flies, swarms of them, coming from nowhere, settled on it.

'AND NO BIRD SINGS'

THE red chimneys of the house for which I was bound were visible from just outside the station at which I had alighted, and, so the chauffeur told me, the distance was not more than a mile's walk if I took the path across the fields. It ran straight till it came to the edge of that wood yonder, which belonged to my host, and above which his chimneys were visible. I should find a gate in the paling of this wood, and a track traversing it, which debouched close to his garden. So, in this adorable afternoon of early May, it seemed a waste of time to do other than walk through the meadows and woods, and I set off on foot, while the motor carried my traps.

It was one of those golden days which every now and again leak out of Paradise and drip to earth. Spring had been late in coming, but now it was here with a burst, and the whole world was boiling with the sap of life. Never have I seen such a wealth of spring flowers, or such vividness of green, or heard such melodious business among the birds in the hedgerows; this walk through the meadows was a jubilee of festal ecstasy. And best of all, so I promised myself, would be the passage through the wood newly fledged with milky green that lay

137

just ahead. There was the gate, just facing me, and I passed through it into the dappled lights and shadows of the grass-grown track.

Coming out of the brilliant sunshine was like entering a dim tunnel; one had the sense of being suddenly withdrawn from the brightness of the spring into some subaqueous cavern. The tree-tops formed a green roof overhead, excluding the light to a remarkable degree; I moved in a world of shifting obscurity. Presently, as the trees grew more scattered, their place was taken by a thick growth of hazels, which met over the path, and then, the ground sloping downwards, I came upon an open clearing, covered with bracken and heather and studded with birches. But though I now walked once more beneath the luminous sky, with the sunlight pouring down, it seemed to have lost its effulgence. The brightness – was it some odd optical illusion? – was veiled as if it came through crêpe. Yet there was the sun still well above the tree-tops in an unclouded heaven, but for all that the light was that of a stormy winter's day, without warmth or brilliance. It was oddly silent, too; I had thought that the bushes and trees would be ringing with the song of mating birds, but listening, I could hear no note of any sort, neither the fluting of thrush or blackbird, nor the cheerful whirr of the chaffinch, nor the cooing wood-pigeon, nor the strident clamour of the jay. I paused to verify this odd silence; there was no doubt about it.

It was rather eerie, rather uncanny, but I supposed the birds knew their own business best, and if they were too busy to sing it was their affair.

As I went on it struck me also that since entering the wood I had not seen a bird of any kind; and now, as I crossed the clearing, I kept my eyes alert for them, but fruitlessly, and soon I entered the further belt of thick trees which surrounded it. Most of them I noticed were beeches, growing very close to each other, and the ground beneath them was bare but for the carpet of fallen leaves, and a few thin bramble-bushes. In this curious dimness and thickness of the trees, it was impossible to see far to right or left of the path, and now, for the first time since I had left the open, I heard some sound of life. There came the rustle of leaves from not far away, and I thought to myself that a rabbit, anyhow, was moving. But somehow it lacked the staccato patter of a small animal; there was a certain stealthy heaviness about it, as if something much larger were stealing along and desirous of not being heard. I paused again to see what might emerge, but instantly the sound ceased. Simultaneously I was conscious of some faint but very foul odour reaching me, a smell choking and corrupt, yet somehow pungent, more like the odour of something alive rather than rotting. It was peculiarly sickening, and not wanting to get any closer to its source I went on my way.

Before long I came to the edge of the wood; straight in

front of me was a strip of meadow-land, and beyond an iron gate between two brick walls, through which I had a glimpse of lawn and flower-beds. To the left stood the house, and over house and garden there poured the amazing brightness of the declining afternoon.

Hugh Granger and his wife were sitting out on the lawn, with the usual pack of assorted dogs: a Welsh collie, a yellow retriever, a fox-terrier, and a Pekinese. Their protest at my intrusion gave way to the welcome of recognition, and I was admitted into the circle. There was much to say, for I had been out of England for the last three months, during which time Hugh had settled into this little estate left him by a recluse uncle, and he and Daisy had been busy during the Easter vacation with getting into the house. Certainly it was a most attractive legacy; the house, through which I was presently taken, was a delightful little Queen Anne manor, and its situation on the edge of this heather-clad Surrey ridge quite superb. We had tea in a small panelled parlour overlooking the garden, and soon the wider topics narrowed down to those of the day and the hour. I had walked, had I, asked Daisy, from the station: did I go through the wood, or follow the path outside it?

The question she thus put to me was given trivially enough; there was no hint in her voice that it mattered a straw to her which way I had come. But it was quite clearly borne in upon me that not only she but Hugh also listened intently for my reply. He had just lit a match for his cigarette, but held it unapplied till he heard my answer. Yes, I had gone through the wood; but now, though I had received some odd impressions in the wood, it seemed quite ridiculous to mention what they were. I could not soberly say that the sunshine there was of very poor quality, and that at one point in my traverse I had smelt a most iniquitous odour. I had walked through the wood; that was all I had to tell them.

I had known both my host and hostess for a tale of many years, and now, when I felt that there was nothing except purely fanciful stuff that I could volunteer about my experiences there, I noticed that they exchanged a swift glance, and could easily interpret it. Each of them signalled to the other an expression of relief; they told each other (so I construed their glance) that I, at any rate, had found nothing unusual in the wood, and they were pleased at that. But then, before any real pause had succeeded to my answer that I had gone through the wood, I remembered that strange absence of bird-song and birds, and as that seemed an innocuous observation in natural history, I thought I might as well mention it.

'One odd thing struck me,' I began (and instantly I saw the attention of both riveted again), 'I didn't see a single bird or hear one from the time I entered the wood to when I left it.'

Hugh lit his cigarette.

'I've noticed that too,' he said, 'and it's rather puzzling. The wood is certainly a bit of primeval forest, and one would have thought that hosts of birds would have nested in it from time immemorial. But, like you, I've never heard or seen one in it. And I've never seen a rabbit there either.'

'I thought I heard one this afternoon,' said I. 'Something was moving in the fallen beech leaves.'

'Did you see it?' he asked.

I recollected that I had decided that the noise was not quite the patter of a rabbit.

'No, I didn't see it,' I said, 'and perhaps it wasn't one. It sounded, I remember, more like something larger.'

Once again and unmistakingly a glance passed between Hugh and his wife, and she rose.

'I must be off,' she said. 'Post goes out at seven, and I lazed all morning. What are you two going to do?'

'Something out of doors, please,' said I. 'I want to see the domain.'

Hugh and I accordingly strolled out again with the cohort of dogs. The domain was certainly very charming; a small lake lay beyond the garden, with a reed bed vocal with warblers, and a tufted margin into which coots and moorhens scudded at our approach. Rising from the end of that was a high heathery knoll full of rabbit holes, which the dogs nosed at with joyful expectations, and there we sat for a while over-looking the wood which covered the rest of the estate. Even now in the blaze of the sun near to its setting, it seemed to be in shadow, though like the rest of the view it should have basked in brilliance, for not a cloud flecked the sky and the level rays enveloped the world in a crimson splendour. But the wood was grey and darkling. Hugh, also, I was aware, had been looking at it, and now, with an air of breaking into a disagreeable topic, he turned to me.

'Tell me,' he said, 'does anything strike you about that wood?'

'Yes: it seems to lie in shadow.'

He frowned.

'But it can't, you know,' he said. 'Where does the shadow come from? Not from outside, for sky and land are on fire.'

'From inside, then?' I asked.

He was silent a moment.

'There's something queer about it,' he said at length. 'There's something there, and I don't know what it is. Daisy feels it too; she won't ever go into the wood, and it appears that birds won't either. Is it just the fact that, for some un-explained reason, there are no birds in it that has set all our imaginations at work?'

I jumped up.

'Oh, it's all rubbish,' I said. 'Let's go through it now and find a bird. I bet you I find a bird.'

'Sixpence for every bird you see,' said Hugh.

We went down the hillside and walked round the wood till we came to the gate where I had entered that afternoon. I held it open after I had gone in for the dogs to follow. But there they stood, a yard or so away, and none of them moved.

'Come on, dogs,' I said, and Fifi, the fox-terrier, came a step nearer and then with a little whine retreated again.

'They always do that,' said Hugh, 'not one of them will set foot inside the wood. Look!'

He whistled and called, he cajoled and scolded, but it was no use. There the dogs remained, with little apologetic grins and signallings of tails, but quite determined not to come.

'But why?' I asked.

'Same reason as the birds, I suppose, whatever that happens to be. There's Fifi, for instance, the sweetest-tempered little lady; once I tried to pick her up and carry her in, and she snapped at me. They'll have nothing to do with the wood; they'll trot round outside it and go home.'

We left them there, and in the sunset light which was now beginning to fade began the passage. Usually the sense of eeriness disappears if one has a companion, but now to me, even with Hugh walking by my side, the place seemed even more uncanny than it had done that afternoon, and a sense of intolerable uneasiness, that grew into a sort of waking nightmare, obsessed me. I had thought before that the silence and loneliness of it had played tricks with my nerves; but with Hugh here it could not be that, and indeed I felt that it was not any such notion that lay at the root of this fear, but rather the conviction that there was some presence lurking there, invisible as yet, but permeating the gathered gloom. I could not form the slightest idea of what it might be, or whether it was material or ghostly; all I could diagnose of it from my own sensations was that it was evil and antique.

As we came to the open ground in the middle of the wood, Hugh stopped, and though the evening was cool I noticed that he mopped his forehead.

'Pretty nasty,' he said. 'No wonder the dogs don't like it. How do you feel about it?'

Before I could answer, he shot out his hand, pointing to the belt of trees that lay beyond.

'What's that?' he said in a whisper.

I followed his finger, and for one half-second thought I saw against the black of the wood some vague flicker, grey or faintly luminous. It waved as if it had been the head and forepart of some huge snake rearing itself, but it instantly disappeared, and my glimpse had been so momentary that I could not trust my impression.

'It's gone,' said Hugh, still looking in the direction he had pointed; and as we stood there, I heard again what I had heard that afternoon, a rustle among the fallen beech-leaves. But there was no wind nor breath of breeze astir.

He turned to me.

'What on earth was it?' he said. 'It looked like some enormous slug standing up. Did you see it?'

'I'm not sure whether I did or not,' I said. 'I think I just caught sight of what you saw.'

'But what was it?' he said again. 'Was it a real material creature, or was it——'

'Something ghostly, do you mean?' I asked.

'Something halfway between the two,' he said. 'I'll tell you what I mean afterwards, when we've got out of this place.'

The thing, whatever it was, had vanished among the trees to the left of where our path lay, and in silence we walked across the open till we came to where it entered tunnel-like among the trees. Frankly I hated and feared the thought of plunging into that darkness with the knowledge that not so far off there was something the nature of which I could not ever so faintly conjecture, but which, I now made no doubt, was that which filled the wood with some nameless terror. Was it material, was it ghostly, or was it (and now some inkling of what Hugh meant began to form itself into my mind) some being that lay on the borderline between the two? Of all the sinister possibilities that appeared the most terrifying.

As we entered the trees again I perceived that reek, alive

and yet corrupt, which I had smelt before, but now it was far more potent, and we hurried on, choking with the odour that I now guessed to be not the putrescence of decay, but the living substance of that which crawled and reared itself in the darkness of the wood where no bird would shelter. Somewhere among those trees lurked the reptilian thing that defied and yet compelled credence.

It was a blessed relief to get out of that dim tunnel into the wholesome air of the open and the clear light of evening. Within doors, when we returned, windows were curtained and lamps lit. There was a hint of frost, and Hugh put a match to the fire in his room, where the dogs, still a little apologetic, hailed us with thumpings of drowsy tails.

'And now we've got to talk,' said he, 'and lay our plans, for whatever it is that is in the wood, we've got to make an end of it. And, if you want to know what I think it is, I'll tell you.'

'Go ahead,' said I.

'You may laugh at me, if you like,' he said, 'but I believe it's an elemental. That's what I meant when I said it was a being halfway between the material and the ghostly. I never caught a glimpse of it till this afternoon; I only felt there was something horrible there. But now I've seen it, and it's like what spiritualists and that sort of folk describe as an elemental. A huge phosphorescent slug is what they tell us of it, which at will can surround itself with darkness.'

Somehow, now safe within doors, in the cheerful light and warmth of the room, the suggestion appeared merely grotesque. Out there in the darkness of that uncomfortable wood something within me had quaked, and I was prepared to believe any horror, but now commonsense revolted.

'But you don't mean to tell me you believe in such rubbish?' I said. 'You might as well say it was a unicorn. What *is* an elemental, anyway? Who has ever seen one except the people who listen to raps in the darkness and say they are made by their aunts?'

'What is it then?' he asked.

'I should think it is chiefly our own nerves,' I said. 'I frankly acknowledge I got the creeps when I went through the wood first, and I got them much worse when I went through it with you. But it was just nerves; we are frightening ourselves and each other.'

'And are the dogs frightening themselves and each other?' he asked. 'And the birds?'

That was rather harder to answer; in fact I gave it up.

Hugh continued.

'Well, just for the moment we'll suppose that something else, not ourselves, frightened us and the dogs and the birds,' he said, 'and that we did see something like a huge phosphorescent slug. I won't call it an elemental, if you object to that; I'll call it It. There's another thing, too, which the existence of

148

It would explain.'

'What's that?' I asked.

'Well, It is supposed to be some incarnation of evil; it is a corporeal form of the devil. It is not only spiritual, it is material to this extent that it can be seen bodily in form, and heard, and, as you noticed, smelt, and, God forbid, handled. It has to be kept alive by nourishment. And that explains perhaps why, every day since I have been here, I've found on that knoll we went up some half-dozen dead rabbits.'

'Stoats and weasels,' said I.

'No, not stoats and weasels. Stoats kill their prey and eat it. These rabbits have not been eaten; they've been drunk.'

'What on earth do you mean?' I asked.

'I examined several of them. There was just a small hole in their throats, and they were drained of blood. Just skin and bones, and a sort of grey mash of fibre, like, like the fibre of an orange which has been sucked. Also there was a horrible smell lingering on them. And was the thing you had a glimpse of like a stoat or a weasel?'

There came a rattle at the handle of the door.

'Not a word to Daisy,' said Hugh as she entered.

'I heard you come in,' she said. 'Where did you go?'

'All round the place,' said I, 'and came back through the wood. It is odd; not a bird did we see, but that is partly accounted for because it was dark.'

I saw her eyes search Hugh's, but she found no communi-
cation there. I guessed that he was planning some attack on
It next day, and he did not wish her to know that anything
was afoot.

'The wood's unpopular,' he said. 'Birds won't go there,
dogs won't go there, and Daisy won't go there. I'm bound to
say I share the feeling too, but having braved its terrors in the
dark I've broken the spell.'

'All quiet, was it?' asked she.

'Quiet wasn't the word for it. The smallest pin could have
been heard dropping half a mile off.'

We talked over our plans that night after she had gone up
to bed. Hugh's story about the sucked rabbits was rather horrible, and though there was no certain connection between
those empty rinds of animals and what we had seen, there
seemed a certain reasonableness about it. But anything, as he
pointed out, which could feed like that was clearly not without its material side – ghosts did not have dinner, and if it was
material it was vulnerable.

Our plans, therefore, were very simple; we were going to
tramp through the wood, as one walks up partridges in a field
of turnips, each with a shot-gun and a supply of cartridges. I
cannot say that I looked forward to the expedition, for I hated
the thought of getting into closer quarters with that mysterious denizen of the woods; but there was a certain excitement

about it, sufficient to keep me awake a long time, and when I got to sleep to cause very vivid and awful dreams.

The morning failed to fulfil the promise of the clear sunset; the sky was lowering and cloudy and a fine rain was falling. Daisy had shopping-errands which took her into the little town, and as soon as she had set off we started on our business. The yellow retriever, mad with joy at the sight of guns, came bounding with us across the garden, but on our entering the wood he slunk back home again.

The wood was roughly circular in shape, with a diameter perhaps of half a mile. In the centre, as I have said, there was an open clearing about a quarter of a mile across, which was thus surrounded by a belt of thick trees and copse a couple of hundred yards in breadth. Our plan was first to walk together up the path which led through the wood, with all possible stealth, hoping to hear some movement on the part of what we had come to seek. Failing that, we had settled to tramp through the wood at the distance of some fifty yards from each other in a circular track; two or three of these circuits would cover the whole ground pretty thoroughly. Of the nature of our quarry, whether it would try to steal away from us, or possibly attack, we had no idea; it seemed, however, yesterday to have avoided us.

Rain had been falling steadily for an hour when we entered to wood; it hissed a little in the tree-tops overhead; but so thick was the cover that the ground below was still not more than damp. It was a dark morning outside; here you would say that the sun had already set and that night was falling. Very quietly we moved up the grassy path, where our footfalls were noiseless, and once we caught a whiff of that odour of live corruption; but though we stayed and listened not a sound of anything stirred except the sibilant rain over our heads. We went across the clearing and through to the far gate, and still there was no sign.

'We'll be getting into the trees then,' said Hugh. 'We had better start where we got that whiff of it.'

We went back to the place, which was towards the middle of the encompassing trees. The odour still lingered on the windless air.

'Go on about fifty yards,' he said, 'and then we'll go in. If either of us comes on the track of it we'll shout to each other.'

I walked on down the path till I had gone the right distance, signalled to him, and we stepped in among the trees.

I have never known the sensation of such utter loneliness. I knew that Hugh was walking parallel with me, only fifty yards away, and if I hung on my step I could faintly hear his tread among the beech leaves. But I felt as if I was quite sundered in this dim place from all companionship of man; the only live thing that lurked here was that monstrous mysterious creature of evil. So thick were the trees that I could not see more than a dozen yards in any direction; all places outside the wood seemed infinitely remote, and infinitely remote also everything that had occurred to me in normal human life. I had been whisked out of all wholesome experiences into this antique and evil place. The rain had ceased, it whispered no longer in the tree-tops, testifying that there did exist a world and a sky outside, and only a few drops from above pattered on the beech leaves.

Suddenly I heard the report of Hugh's gun, followed by his shouting voice.

'I've missed it,' he shouted, 'it's coming in your direction.'

I heard him running towards me, the beech-leaves rustling, and no doubt his footsteps drowned a stealthier noise that was close to me. All that happened now, until once more I heard the report of Hugh's gun, happened, I suppose, in less than a minute. If it had taken much longer I do not imagine I should be telling it today.

I stood there then, having heard Hugh's shout, with my gun cocked, and ready to put to my shoulder, and I listened to his running footsteps. But still I saw nothing to shoot at and heard nothing. Then between two beech trees, quite close to me, I saw what I can only describe as a ball of darkness. It rolled very swiftly towards me over the few yards that separated me from it, and then, too late, I heard the dead beech-leaves rustling below it. Just before it reached me, my brain realised what it was, or what it might be, but before I could raise my gun to shoot at that nothingness, it was upon me. My gun was twitched out of my hand, and I was enveloped in this blackness, which was the very essence of corruption. It knocked me off my feet, and I sprawled flat on my back, and upon me, as I lay there, I felt the weight of this invisible assailant.

I groped wildly with my hands and they clutched something cold and slimy and hairy. They slipped off it, and next moment there was laid across my shoulder and neck something which felt like an india-rubber tube. The end of it fastened on to my neck like a snake, and I felt the skin rise beneath it. Again, with clutching hands, I tried to tear that obscene strength away from me, and as I struggled with it, I heard Hugh's footsteps close to me through this layer of darkness that hid everything.

My mouth was free, and I shouted at him.

'Here, here!' I yelled. 'Close to you, where it is darkest.'

I felt his hands on mine, and that added strength detached from my neck that sucker that pulled at it. The coil that lay heavy on my legs and chest writhed and struggled and relaxed. Whatever it was that our four hands held, slipped out of them and I saw Hugh standing close to me. A yard or two off, vanishing among the beech trunks, was that darkness which had poured over me. Hugh put up his gun, and with his second barrel fired at it.

The blackness dispersed, and there, wriggling and twisting like a huge worm lay what we had come to find. It was alive still, and I picked up my gun which lay by my side and fired two more barrels into it. The writhings dwindled into mere shudderings and shakings, and then it lay still.

With Hugh's help I got to my feet, and we both reloaded before going nearer. On the ground there lay a monstrous thing, half slug, half worm. There was no head to it; it ended in a blunt point with an orifice. In colour it was grey covered with sparse black hairs; its length I suppose was some four feet, its thickness at the broadest part was that of a man's thigh, tapering towards each end. It was shattered by shot at its middle. There were stray pellets which had hit it elsewhere, and from the holes they had made there oozed not blood, but some grey viscous matter.

As we stood there some swift process of disintegration and decay began. It lost outline, it melted, it liquefied, and in a minute more we were looking at a mass of stained and coagulated beech leaves. Again and quickly that liquor of corruption faded, and there lay at our feet no trace of what had been there. The overpowering odour passed away, and there came from the ground just the sweet savour of wet earth in springtime, and from above the glint of a sunbeam piercing the clouds. Then a sudden pattering among the dead leaves sent my heart into my mouth again, and I cocked my gun. But it was only Hugh's yellow retriever who had joined us.

We looked at each other.

'You're not hurt?' he said.

I held my chin up.

'Not a bit,' I said. 'The skin's not broken, is it?'

'No; only a round red mark. My God, what was it? What happened?'

'Your turn first,' said I. 'Begin at the beginning.'

'I came upon it quite suddenly,' he said. 'It was lying coiled like a sleeping dog behind a big beech. Before I could fire, it slithered off in the direction where I knew you were. I got a snap shot at it among the trees, but I must have missed, for I heard it rustling away. I shouted to you and ran after it. There was a circle of absolute darkness on the ground, and your voice came from the middle of it. I couldn't see you at all, but I clutched at the blackness and my hands met yours. They met something else, too.'

We got back to the house and had put the guns away before Daisy came home from her shopping. We had also scrubbed and brushed and washed. She came into the smoking-room.

'You lazy folk,' she said. 'It has cleared up, and why are you still indoors? Let's go out at once.'

I got up.

'Hugh has told me you've got a dislike of the wood,' I said, 'and it's a lovely wood. Come and see; he and I will walk on each side of you and hold your hands. The dogs shall protect you as well.'

'But not one of them will go a yard into the wood,' said she.

'Oh yes, they will. At least we'll try them. You must promise to come if they do.'

Hugh whistled them up, and down we went to the gate. They sat panting for it to be opened, and scuttled into the thickets in pursuit of interesting smells.

'And who says there are no birds in it?' said Daisy. 'Look at that robin! Why, there are two of them. Evidently house-hunting.'